"I'm Sorry," Kane Said Quietly.

With the feathery touch of his finger still burning her skin, Rory couldn't think of a word to say. It took all her strength not to walk into those warm, friendly arms and stay there for the rest of her life.

"It's not your fault," she said, not sure of anything except how she felt about her fiancé's best man.

He had kissed her. She was still reeling from it. That wide, crooked mouth had touched hers, and now all she could think of was the way he tasted, the way he felt against her body, all hard and warm and exciting.

She looked away, embarrassed at what she was thinking, hoping Kane had forgotten about kissing her. Hoping even more that he hadn't. Hoping that her husband-to-be would learn to kiss the way Kane did....

Dear Reader,

Welcome to August! As I promised last month, August's *Man of the Month* title is by one of your favorites—and mine—Diana Palmer. It's called *Night of Love,* and this story really is something wonderful and special.

The rest of August is equally terrific. First, there's *Kane's Way* by Dixie Browning. You know, it's hard to believe that this talented lady has written over *fifty* books for Silhouette! And they all just keep getting better and better.

Next comes a fun-filled story from Lass Small. The title of Lass's latest is *Balanced,* but I'm not sure that our hero and heroine feel exactly "balanced" for most of the book ... more like *off*-balanced from love.

The month is completed by delightful, sensuous, sparkling stories from Cathie Linz, Linda Turner and Barbara McCauley. And as for September, well, have we got some great stuff in store for you. Look for new series by Ann Major *and* Joan Hohl, as well as some delightful tales from four other fabulous writers.

So, until next month, happy reading.

Lucia Macro
Senior Editor

DIXIE BROWNING

KANE'S WAY

SILHOUETTE *Desire*®

Published by Silhouette Books New York

America's Publisher of Contemporary Romance

SILHOUETTE BOOKS
300 East 42nd St., New York, N.Y. 10017

KANE'S WAY

ISBN: 0-373-05801-2

First Silhouette Books printing August 1993

All the characters in this book have no existence outside the imagination of the author and have no relation whatsoever to anyone bearing the same name or names. They are not even distantly inspired by any individual known or unknown to the author, and all incidents are pure invention.

Books by Dixie Browning

Silhouette Desire

Shadow of Yesterday #68
Image of Love #91
The Hawk and the Honey #111
Late Rising Moon #121
Stormwatch #169
The Tender Barbarian #188
Matchmaker's Moon #212
A Bird in the Hand #234
In the Palm of Her Hand #264
A Winter Woman #324
There Once Was a Lover #337
Fate Takes a Holiday #403
Along Came Jones #427
Thin Ice #474
Beginner's Luck #517
Ships in the Night #541
Twice in a Blue Moon #588
Just Say Yes #637
Not a Marrying Man #678
Gus and the Nice Lady #691
Best Man for the Job #720
Hazards of the Heart #780
Kane's Way #801

Silhouette Books

Silhouette Christmas Stories 1987
"Henry the Ninth"

Silhouette Romance

Unreasonable Summer #12
Tumbled Wall #38
Chance Tomorrow #53
Wren of Paradise #73
East of Today #93
Winter Blossom #113
Renegade Player #142
Island on the Hill #164
Logic of the Heart #172
Loving Rescue #191
A Secret Valentine #203
Practical Dreamer #221
Visible Heart #275
Journey to Quiet Waters #292
The Love Thing #305
First Things Last #323
Something for Herself #381
Reluctant Dreamer #460
A Matter of Timing #527
The Homing Instinct #747

Silhouette Special Edition

Finders Keepers #50
Reach Out To Cherish #110
Just Deserts #181
Time and Tide #205
By Any Other Name #228
The Security Man #314
Belonging #414

DIXIE BROWNING

has written over fifty books for Silhouette since 1980. She is a charter member of the Romance Writers of America and an award-winning author, and has toured extensively for Silhouette Books. She also writes historical romances with her sister under the name Bronwyn Williams.

To Isabel Swift,
for all the good years

Prologue

It could have been fate. It could've been boredom. It could have been a few too many industrial-strength margaritas.

Or it could have been the combination of all those things, plus the coincidence of hearing that old classic melody about flying purple people eaters, that brought on the final stages of acute nostalgia.

Kane slid down to the end of the bar, where the cord from the wall-mounted pay phone would reach, and dialed 919 information. It had been eleven years since he'd seen old Charlie standing outside the church with his arms around Suzanne, while the photographer snapped their pictures.

Kane hadn't stuck around for the postnuptial festivities. He had sent Christmas cards to Mr. and Mrs. for the first few years, but never included a return address. Knowing Charlie, he would still be living in that same old house on Tobaccoville Road. Men like Charles Edward William Banks III—or was that William Edward?—always lived in houses some worthy male ancestor had built. Men like ol' Charlie always married the prettiest lady in town and lived happily ever after, while men like Kane Smith lived on adrenaline, and a ready supply of redheads—preferably the dark-eyed variety, with rosy cheeks, red lips and pale pink nipples.

By now, the two of them probably had a houseful of kids. All Kane had, he reminded himself lugubriously, was a bad back—relic of a hasty ejection over the Persian Gulf, incipient cataracts from staring into the sun for too many years and, just lately, a couple of books on the *New York Times* bestseller list. Was that fair?

Hell no, it wasn't fair! "Yeah, that's right operator. Tobaccoville. It's near King, near, uh...how about Rural Hall?" By the time he got around to mentioning Winston-Salem, the phone was ringing on the other end.

Kane sat up straighter, blinking to focus his eyes. "Charlie? Is that you, ol' man? Hey, you remember the time the three of us, you'n me an' Suzanne, drove out to that place west of Chapel Hill and spent eleven dollars playing 'Flying Purple People Eater' on the jukebox?"

"I beg your p— Who *is* this?"

"Did I ever tell you what a real son of a bitch you were for takin' her 'way from me, Charlie?"

"Kane? Is that you?"

"The parts of me I can still feel seem sorta familiar. Not too sure about m'nose and feet. Think they b'long to somebody else. Charlie, d'you think you could poss'bly come down here and drive me home? My body's been taken over by aliens."

"Kane, where are you?"

"I'm right here, Charlie, where're you?"

"Oh, for heaven's sake, you haven't changed a bit, have you? Still the same irresponsible, reckless, child-ish—"

"Child*less,* Charlie, not child—*iss*...childish," Kane repeated carefully. "D'you have children, Charlie? Did Suzanne breast-feed your babies? I could've had me a woman with a bunch o' babies all over 'er breasts, Charlie. Zanne should've married me instead o' you. I loved her, Charlie, I really did, only she broke my heart an' married you instead, an' I've never looked at an-other woman, I swear it, Charlie, I swear to you I've never—"

"You're drunk."

"Well, o' course I'm drunk," Kane said indignantly. "D'you think I'd talk to the bastard who stole my woman if I was sober?"

Kane blinked away a sudden film of tears. "Ah, Charlie, you're the lucky one. You may be a real pain in the back seat, but at leas' you've got a woman to warm the cockerels—the cocker—to warm your bed, and li'l kiddies to drool all over your shoes an' wipe cookie crumbs on your nice gray suits."

"Kane, Suzanne d—"

"Me, I got nothing. Zip. Zilch. *Nada.* I can't fly anymore, did I tell you that, Charlie? No wings. No more Apaches, no more Desert Storm, no more return-nin' hero. An' Charlie, you know what's got me so scared I can't even sh—"

"Kane, I'm not going to listen to any more of your drunken ramblings. Now you go home and sober up and then if you want to call me tomorrow, we'll discuss things in a rational, civilized manner. I'll be at the office until—"

"I'll tell you what's got me scared, my frien'—my bes' frien', my ol' buddy, my chil'hood pal. I'm lonesome. Pillow-huggin', hollow-belly, howl-at-the-moon lonesome, tha's what I am. I came down here with a bee-yoo-tiful redhead, an' I can't even get it on, an' you know why? I'll tell you why, Charlie, 'cause it's all your fault. Th' only woman I ever loved—"

"Kane, we were so young for pity sake, and besides, Suzanne d—"

"—Married my bes' frien' and I'm sittin' here in a bar in Key Wes' all by myself, and I— Wha' was the question?"

"Where are you staying? No, I don't want to hear 'Flying Purple People Eater' on the jukebox, Kane. Just tell me where you're staying, and I'll call you in the morning."

Rory pursed her lips and dabbed on a hint of coral lipstick with the tip of her little finger. Charles didn't care for too much makeup. He was taking her out to a new restaurant tonight instead of the same old club, and she was determined to have a good time.

The restaurant was crowded. Charles was frowning by the time they were shown to their table.

"You must have had a difficult day," she murmured.

"My work is vitally important, Aurora. I can't just shake it off when I walk out the office door, you know."

"No, I know you can't, dear." Soothing Charles was a habit, but she was determined to enjoy the break in their usual routine. She ordered curried scallops on a bed of fettucini with a tahini sauce.

Charles lifted his pale eyebrows. He ordered broiled chicken breast. "That's always safe," he remarked.

Hands clasped tightly together in her lap, Rory changed her order. Charles was right, of course. There was no point in courting disaster when one already had a nervous stomach.

At 9:37, Charles parked in his own driveway and walked her to the front porch of the bungalow next door, where he left her with a sweet, brief kiss. His kisses were really rather pleasant, not at all demanding. But then one of the things Rory liked best about Charles Banks was that he was not a demanding man, despite the fact that he had been married before, and men who had been married were reputed to take sex for granted.

Charles had told her at the beginning of their courtship that Suzanne had been the love of his life. However, Suzanne was dead, and now Charles wanted a marriage based on shared interests, shared responsibilities and shared respect, which suited Rory perfectly. She wasn't the type of woman who could ever enjoy one of those messy, stormy relationships that entailed all sorts of... intimacies.

She was lucky to have found a man like Charles, who, while he might be somewhat dull and even a bit of a chauvinist at times, was also handsome, kind and successful. The sort of man her grandmother would have approved of.

On Saturday night they went to the club for dinner. Charles had played golf there all afternoon with a client. Rory didn't play golf, which hardly mattered, for as Charles said, second-grade teachers seldom needed to court clients.

They talked about a new local ordinance. They discussed Charles's flawlessly landscaped backyard, which Rory was itching to get her hands on as soon as they were married. They talked about what Charles's dentist had said about saving his right upper molar.

He ordered calf's liver. She ordered chicken potpie. It was that kind of club.

At the door that night, he kissed her again. Rory invited him in for a second dessert, but he claimed several hours of paperwork still to be done before he could turn in.

"It won't be long now, my dear," Charles said softly, his light blue eyes crinkling at the corners in a way that invited instant trust, an important quality in an insurance broker. "Then I won't have to let you go, ever again." He kissed the diamond engagement ring he had given her three weeks earlier. Rory counted it as a mark of respect that he had waited a full year after Suzanne died to propose. She knew he was lonely in that great big old house. He and the housekeeper, who came in daily, must rattle around in all those rooms. One of the things Rory was looking forward to most was having more space for her various projects.

Charles said, "I'd better go, dear. I promised to call an old friend again tonight. He's at loose ends—but then, he always was. Wild, but a decent sort at heart. Actually, I'm thinking of asking him to stand as best man for our wedding, for old time's sake."

The wedding. Best men. Attendants. Sooner or later she was going to have to make some plans of her own....

"There was a time when Kane and Suzanne and I were close. As a matter of fact, Kane and Suzanne— Well, that's neither here nor there. You'd better get some sleep, my dear, you've been looking rather peaked lately."

He kissed her lightly again, on the mouth this time, and Rory's stomach quivered a warning. She whispered good-night and, once inside, headed directly for the kitchen, where she took a dose of baking soda in water.

That night she had a bad dream and woke herself up making puffy little cries for help.

One

Five days later, Aurora Hubbard was scrubbing her front porch. That in itself was nothing out of the ordinary. Rory was neat and orderly by nature, traits that had been drummed into her by her grandmother.

Besides, she had company coming...probably. Sooner or later.

Kane Smith, restless and alone with his thoughts after too many years of holding the past at bay, wandered outside for a smoke. He wasn't sure it had been such a smart idea, coming back to town to stand by while old Charlie took himself another wife. For one thing, it had been a real shocker, learning about Suzanne's death.

Not that he hadn't lost friends before. Being in a war, even a brief one, those things happened. But this was different. Suzanne had been a part of what Kane liked to think of as the days of innocence. The days before he had gone through hell and come out on the other side a hundred years older, if not a hell of a lot wiser.

They'd spent a couple of hours talking over old times before Charlie had gone up to bed. Kane had gone upstairs, too, but he hadn't been able to sleep. Oh, he had come to terms with the fact of Suzanne's death. He had even come to terms with the fact that the dream he'd been carrying around ever since his college days was worn so thin it bore little resemblance to reality. Suzanne had been a sweet, silly, selfish little redhead, and Kane suspected they would have driven each other nuts within a very short time had he married her.

But she'd been smart enough to dump him for Charlie. Evidently, the pair of them had suited just fine. From all Kane had heard tonight, the new Mrs. Charlie would suit even better. According to Charlie, she was an elementary schoolteacher, well respected in the community. Neat, quiet, serious and sensible, she was well past the stage of expecting a man to act like the hero of a romantic novel.

Neat, quiet and sensible. They sounded like a matched pair of bookends, Kane thought as he wandered out onto the porch. Except in the looks department. Charles had been voted best-looking boy in their senior class. Except for a few more inches around the middle and a slightly loftier forehead, he hadn't changed all that much.

Apologetically he'd explained that his new lady wasn't much to look at. A dishwater blond, he'd said. "Actually, her complexion can't be compared to Suzanne's, either," Charles had admitted. "However, she has quite a nice smile and people seem to like her."

Kane wished them luck. They'd probably bore each other stiff within a month, but that was none of his business.

Mildly curious, because his mother had once rented the same bungalow next door to the Bankses where Charlie's spinster schoolteacher now lived, Kane wandered closer. Same old hedge. Same wisteria threatening to take over the neighborhood. He and Charles used to joke about it being the purple people eater.

He slipped through the same old crack in the hedge that had been trampled indelibly back when the two boys were growing up, and then he stopped short, his eyes narrowed against the glare of a naked yellow bulb.

This was Charlie's neat, sensible schoolteacher?

Kane pushed up the cuff of his khaki shirt and glanced at his battered stainless-steel watch. It was precisely twenty-two minutes past midnight. The woman was on her hands and knees, scrubbing her front porch. Either Kane was hallucinating or she had flipped out.

Or maybe Charlie had flipped out.

Nah. Charlie wasn't the type to flip out over a woman. An incorrectly filed form, maybe. Or a tie that clashed with his suit. But Charlie would never knowingly get mixed up with a midnight porch scrubber. His mama would pitch a royal fit. Kane remembered that lady all too well from having grown up in the house next door. The arbiter of all things social in the small town of Tobaccoville, North Carolina, Madeline Banks had made life hell for the wild rebel Kane had been in those days. The more she had called him a bad influence and forbade her Charles to associate with him, the more determined the two boys had been to stick together. With Kane taking the lead—and usually the blame—the two of them had sampled some of life's finest pleasures. Fast cars, fast boats, fast women and cheap wine.

But in the end, breeding won out. Charles had followed his father into the insurance business, while Kane had gone his own way.

Funny that he should be back here again and for the same reason—to stand up with Charlie while he tied the knot. Eleven years, Kane mused. A lot could change in eleven years.

He watched as the woman, her tidy little stern twitching a counterrhythm to her shoulders, scoured the devil out of the battleship-gray-painted floor. She tackled a spot of dirt, paused, sighed, lowered her forearms on the floor, and then rested her forehead on her crossed wrists.

Charlie had said his fiancée had rented the house from him when she'd first moved to Tobaccoville and that she lived alone. Was there a moonlighting maid service around these parts?

Nah...she had to be Charlie's woman. But did Charlie know about her secret vice? Did *she* know about Charlie's passion for hidebound, conventional decorum? It was damned near the only passion he had, as far as Kane had ever been able to determine.

The kind of woman Charlie had described wouldn't be caught dead on her knees in the middle of the night unless she was praying. Certainly not on a front porch with a scrub brush in her hands.

Or in a bedroom with something more interesting in her hands.

Congenitally drawn to anything that hinted at a puzzle, Kane moved closer, his footsteps silent on the dew-damp grass. He was halfway to the porch when the woman heaved another hard sigh, levered herself up and commenced scrubbing again. From the shadow of an overhanging oak, he continued to watch, no longer bored, no longer restless.

She was wearing the kind of cotton pajamas designed specifically to squelch any salacious notions. Under the yellow bug light, Kane couldn't be sure of the color, but one thing he was becoming more certain of by the minute—any marriage between this woman and Charles William Edward Banks III, was going to self-destruct within a short time unless he was very much mistaken.

Intrigued, Kane moved silently on the damp grass until he was only a few feet away. Not that he was trying to be stealthy, but how the hell was a strange man supposed to approach an even stranger woman under circumstances like these?

What was her name, anyway? Charlie had mentioned it. Something with an *R* that ended in *A*. Ramona? Victoria?

He grinned. If this lady had a single Victorian bone in her twitching little body, it sure as hell wasn't apparent from this angle.

Thoroughly enjoying himself, Kane watched her erratic backward progress. Under the yellow light, her pj's were the color of the Saudi desert. As for her hair, he couldn't tell too much, but offhand, he'd be inclined to say that dishwater blond didn't even come close. Her face, too, was a mystery, but then Kane thrived on mysteries. Or to put it more accurately, he made his living with them.

Kane Smith, ex-flyer, ex-Tarheel, ex-husband—if you counted six miserable months of wedded hell with a gorgeous redheaded lawyer—had just seen his third mystery published. The first one had unexpectedly gone into three printings and made it halfway up the best-seller lists, the second one had hit the top and hovered there for five weeks. Kane had every reason to believe his third novel, due out shortly, would follow suit.

Since his early days at Seymour Johnson AFB, Kane had avoided his home state through no particular design. He'd been living in Cape May since he'd resigned his commission shortly after the Gulf War, but when he was feeling driven—he drove. Sometimes he drove alone, sometimes he found a companion. This time he'd wound up in Key West with a redheaded Vegas show-girl. The girl had been a mistake from day one. He'd bought her a diamond watch and a first-class ticket back to Nevada and deliberately set out to drink his blues away.

And then he'd heard that damned song and called Charlie, and now here he was, staring down at the rear end of a strange female in the small hours of the morning, prey to a variety of emotions that included surprise, curiosity and an unexpected, not to mention inappropriate, rush of arousal.

Was that a piece of *string* tied around her right ankle?

Oblivious to the man staring down at her backside, Rory moved the brush in halfhearted circles. Thirteen more days of freedom. She sighed and lowered her head to her crossed wrists again. Four weeks from now, school would be in session and she was going to have to instruct a roomful of children who knew her as Miss Hubbard to start calling her Mrs. Banks. Suddenly that task took on gargantuan proportions.

But then for the past few weeks, ever since she had agreed to marry Charles, even the smallest decision seemed to assume gargantuan proportions. Every little molehill suddenly loomed like Mount Everest. Her nails were chewed off up to the elbows, she was overcaffeinated, her brain alternately raced like a gerbil on a treadmill or shut down completely. This just wasn't like her! Rory had always been the sensible member of her family.

Which, she thought with another sigh, wasn't saying a whole lot.

She had been lying awake worrying about her underwear and her name and whether or not to pay for another month's rent, even though she would only be here for another two weeks, and whether or not her entire family was going to descend on her, causing Charles to freak out, when she'd finally given up on sleep and decided to scrub the front porch. All right, so maybe it wasn't the most rational decision to arrive at in the middle of the night. At least it was a decision. That in itself was an improvement.

But by the time she was halfway done, she was more than ready to quit. Her knees hurt. Her arms ached. This was a dumb thing to do in the middle of the night, and if Charles ever learned of it, he'd be horrified!

So now she was tired enough to sleep, but too grungy to go back to bed, yet if she took another shower she'd be wide awake again. In which case she might as well finish the porch. Always finish what you begin. Never put off until tomorrow, et cetera, et cetera, et cetera. She had heard it all a thousand times from age eleven until the day her grandmother had died.

"What about putting off a wedding that's coming at you like a runaway train in a narrow tunnel?" she muttered. *Pipe down, traitor!*

Irritated, Rory slapped the sudsy brush against the floor and in a sudden burst of energy, commenced scouring away at the place in front of the doormat where traffic had worn off most of the paint.

Her movements slowed. Was she legally obligated to repaint the floor before she moved out? Was that the responsibility of the landlord or the tenant?

Maybe she'd better dig out her lease and read it again.

On the other hand, in less than two weeks she would be Mrs. Landlord, so did it really matter?

Wet and knee sore though she was, Rory had to grin. Charles was such a stickler. It was one of the more comforting things about him. He was nice, he was handsome, but best of all, he was utterly dependable. In fact, decorum was his middle name. Never in this world would anyone catch Charles Banks lying on a patch of grass between the curb and the sidewalk on a summer Sunday afternoon just because he liked the view of the bell tower from that particular angle.

Her father would do something like that. He had, in fact, the last time he had visited her at college, while Rory had cringed and pretended not to be with him.

And while another Rory, she admitted reluctantly—one she usually kept hidden in the closet—had thought: what fun to look at the world from a different angle! Like looking at the ceiling and pretending it's the floor and mentally shifting all the furniture around.

She sighed again. Crawling backward, she slowly worked her way toward the edge of the porch. She had done the ends first—the swing end and the other end, where the wisteria threatened to swallow up the gutters and—oh, dear. She had promised Charles faithfully she would prune it back once it stopped blooming, only she hated pruning. It was such a cruel thing to do. Besides, she liked the way it provided a cozy green barrier between her porch and his.

First thing in the morning, she vowed as she scrubbed her way down the last stretch, she would see if she could find the whackers that had been hanging in the garage when she'd moved in.

Meanwhile there was the porch to finish. She had left the part in front of the door until last so that she could get back inside without tracking, and—

"Oh, crud," she muttered, hurling her brush into the bucket. She was scrubbing herself *away* from the door, not up to it! Couldn't she accomplish a single blessed thing anymore without lousing up?

Snatching up the brush, Rory slung pine-scented suds in all directions as she slapped the bristles onto the floorboards and began scrubbing the last few feet of buckling boards, mumbling obscure vows concerning slow boats to China and fast trains to the Himalayas.

Angrily she dug at a patch of chewing gum with the edge of her brush. That would be the little Miller boy across the street. He was six. She would have him next year, and the first thing she intended to teach him was to park his chewing gum behind his left ear where God had intended him to park it if he wasn't going to keep it in his mouth!

That slow boat was beginning to sound better and better. She could get off on the other side of the world, where no one had ever heard of her or Charles, or Hubbard's Heavenly anything! It had a certain allure, it definitely did!

Rory's left knee felt the edge of the porch just as the sole of her right foot came in contact with something warm and solid and rounded where nothing warm and solid and rounded had any business being. She jerked it back and then cautiously extended it again. With the same results.

Kane, bemused by the intervals of furious activity, followed by mutterings, slumps and sighs, had been staring down at what just might be the sweetest set of glutei maximi in captivity. Her pajamas were worn tissue thin on the seat, which meant that she probably ate her breakfast before getting dressed for the day. Probably changed into her pj's after dinner, as well, if she wasn't going out again. An image of a faceless woman rose before his eyes, all steamy soft from a hot bath, and smelling like... pine? No, definitely not pine. Lilac, maybe—or wisteria.

This just might be worth further investigation.

Rory wriggled her toes experimentally, not daring to look back. If this was Charles, then her engagement was finished. Down the tube. R.I.P.

On the other hand, maybe if she crawled back into the house without looking over her shoulder they could both pretend this had never happened. One day they would probably laugh about it.

Carefully Rory began to make her way toward the door. Charles wouldn't laugh at it. If this was Charles, she was going to find herself involved in some pretty embarrassing explanations.

On the other hand, if it was somebody else...

Oh, Lordy. Think, Crystal Aurora Hubbard—think! Do you scream for help and risk waking Charles up and having him race to the rescue, or do you make a dash for the door, lock yourself in and dial 911?

Before she could come to any conclusion, the heels of her hands slipped on the sudsy floor. Awkwardly she flung herself toward the door and grabbed the corner of the screen, whimpering in frustration when it wouldn't open because her prostrate body was in the way. Scrambling backward, she felt her left foot strike the plastic bucket, heard a muffled clatter, a bump, a splash and a gasp. In that order.

"Ah, hell, lady, now look what you've gone and done! I've only got two pairs of jeans with me."

Suspended between terror and curiosity, Rory managed to turn her head enough to look over her shoulder. After a while, she even remembered to breathe.

It wasn't Charles. She wasn't disgraced forever. It was a stranger. If she had a grain of sense she'd be scared out of her gourd, but somehow, dripping dirty scrub water all over, he didn't look terribly threatening.

"Now I'm going to have to strip down before I go back inside, or that pterodactyl next door will kill me for messing up her clean floors."

"*Charles?*" Rory managed to squawk.

"The housekeeper, Mrs. Whatsername."

"Mrs. Mountjoy. You know Charles, then?" She didn't know whether to be sorry or relieved.

"Yeah, I know Charles," the man grumbled in tones of deep disgust. He unbuttoned his shirt and plucked it away from his body, and Rory noticed that he wasn't wearing an undershirt. It occurred to her fleetingly that even on the hottest day of the year, Charles always wore an undershirt. Not that she'd ever actually seen it. Except through the crisp white dress shirts he always wore with his gray suits.

She quickly turned away. "Um . . . you don't seem like—that is, I don't believe I've ever heard Charles mention your name." *You don't even know his name, clunkhead!*

"No? Somehow, that doesn't surprise me."

"Who are you? How can I be sure you know Charles?" Rory thought she'd met all of Charles's friends, but if she had ever in her life met this one, she would have remembered.

"The name's Smith, and you can't. But if it matters, Charlie and I got our first black eyes in the same fight. I was best man at his first wedding after he stole my girl, and now I'm ready to serve again, which might give you some idea of what a prince of a fellow I am."

"No one who really knows Charles calls him Charlie." It was a losing argument, and she knew it. Still on her hands and knees, Rory stared over her shoulder at the man in the shadows. *This* was Charles's old friend who was going to be best man at their wedding in two weeks? This dark and dangerous-looking man with the crooked nose and the crooked mouth and the wicked eyes? This predatory creature, stalking the night in clinging wet jeans and a khaki shirt, belonged to her Charles?

Rory made an effort to reconcile the man before her with the boyhood friend Charles had told her about— the one who was going to be in town for the wedding. If she had thought about him at all, she would have pictured someone like Charles. A short-haired Brookes Brothers type in wing tips and shoulder padding.

This man's hair wasn't long enough to set off her internal alarm bells, but it definitely wasn't short. And if that was shoulder padding under all that wet khaki, then her old anatomy text was sorely in need of revision.

Absently Rory blew a strand of hair off her forehead, trying desperately to ignore the fact that all the secret fantasies she had worked so hard to bury had suddenly come to life and started talking back to her. "So," she said with a forced smile, "Charles said you used to live in my house?"

Kane nodded. He hadn't missed the way her eyes had darted nervously over his body. Was she deliberately being provocative? Did she have any idea how arousing a man found it to know that a woman's eyes were on his body?

Down, boy! This one's spoken for! "Does the third step to the attic still creak?" he asked, ignoring the clammy feel of wet clothing. As an antiaphrodesiac, he could recommend it. "I used to sleep up there. Hot as the devil in the summertime, freezing all winter. Nice in spring and fall, though."

Waiting for her to formulate a reply, Kane examined Charlie's spinster schoolteacher with her dishwater blond hair and her indifferent complexion and came to a few fast conclusions.   Conclusion number one: the guy was an idiot. Conclusion number two: no man deserved a woman he couldn't appreciate.

Charlie was right, this one wasn't up to Suzanne's standard of beauty, but there was something about her...

Actually, she was sort of...

Frowning slightly, Kane added up what he could see of the woman on her knees before him and came up with something slightly less than he would've expected Charlie to settle for, yet something a hell of a lot more than Charlie had led him to expect.

Sexy? Hell, yes! Beautiful? No way. So what was it about her that got to him? The eyes? Yeah, they were nice enough, but under a yellow light he couldn't even be sure of the color. Her hair was somewhere between blond and brown—definitely not red, but not dishwater, either. At the moment it looked more like a squirrel's nest than anything else.

As for her skin, it suddenly dawned on him that those weren't spots that peppered her rather earnest little face, they were freckles. The damned things covered every visible portion of her body!

He wondered about the invisible portions, and shot down the thought before it could get him into trouble. Charlie's lady's private parts were off-limits.

Still, she had a nice mouth, he mused. Wide, mobile, full lower lip. Did old Charlie have the nerve to take full advantage of it, or was he still the same old hidebound puritan he'd always been?

Nose a bit on the short side, Kane mused, continuing the inventory. Chin more than a bit on the stubborn side. But that mouth of hers, it was something else!

"The step still squeaks," she said, startling him back to reality. "I don't use the attic much." Abruptly, she leaned forward, extended her hand, drew it back and wiped it on her pajama top and held it out again. "I'm Charles's fiancée, Aurora Hubbard. How do you do?"

It was the sheer incongruity of the gesture that got to him. Kane's mouth twisted into a smile as he took her small damp hand. What the devil was Charlie going to do with a woman like this? She'd drive him clean up the wall in no time flat. Either that or he'd wind up throttling her. This wasn't going to work. No way. Oil and water. Vinegar and soda. And it was a damned shame, too, because Charlie was a decent fellow who probably deserved a break. For the first twenty-three years of his life, he'd been under Maddie Banks's iron thumb, and then he'd married Suzanne, only to lose her to, of all things in this day and age, viral pneumonia.

Yeah, poor old Charlie deserved whatever happiness he could find for himself, and if this was where he'd found it, more power to him, but Kane had a sneaking suspicion it wasn't going to work out.

"I believe Charles said you were a writer, Mr. Smith? What sort of things do you write?" Rory asked. Courtesy had been drilled into her by her grandmother, but then her grandmother had probably never envisioned a set of circumstances quite like this.

Kane's grin broadened. Was she for real? If so, she was priceless! How many women could sit on their wet behind looking like the tag end of a hard day and politely ask the well-publicized author of the award-winning *Silent Stalks the Hunter* what sort of thing he wrote?

"Um . . . mostly fiction."

Oh, my mercy, Rory thought, more bemused by the moment. When Charles had mentioned that his friend was a writer, she had naturally assumed he wrote the kind of things Charles read—books full of graphs and tables and statistics. Someone like Charles, only not quite as neat and certainly not as handsome. Someone in tweeds, or maybe a rumpled seersucker suit, with graying hair, thin on top and probably too long in the back. With wire-rimmed glasses . . .

Actually, she hadn't given him much thought at all. She'd had other things on her mind. Such as whether or not to uninvite her family while there was still time. Or if they came, which one of her three sisters she should ask to be her attendant. "I'm sure Charles will enjoy having you here, Mr. Smith. He's been working so hard for so long."

"Make that Kane. I expect we'll be seeing right much of each other over the next two weeks." Was she implying that she couldn't pry Charles away from his desk? This funny, sexy, outrageous creature who scrubbed floors at midnight and shook hands with strange men as politely as if she hadn't just doused them with a bucket of cold, dirty water?

Come to think of it, maybe the cold shower hadn't been such a bad idea. He'd been getting a little too enthusiastic over that trim rear end twitching its way across the porch.

"I reckon you think it's crazy, my scrubbing a porch at this time of night."

"Never entered my mind. I do some of my best work at night."

"Oh." Rory let it drop. Sitting there, with one knee drawn up and both hands spread out behind her, she stared at a slow-drying puddle over near the edge of the porch where the boards dipped.

Neither of them spoke. Rory sighed. Kane wondered why the hell he didn't just walk away.

She had a crumpled tissue in her shirt pocket. The sight of it lumping the thin material over her right breast struck him as incredibly intimate. He pulled the cold, wet cloth away from his own chest and let it flop back again as he continued to study her from the shadows of the shaggy wisteria vine. On closer examination, he thought her hair would be more blond than brown. Pity she wasn't a redhead.

On second thought, maybe it was a damned good thing she wasn't. Kane had always had a weakness for redheads, and the way this woman was beginning to affect him, the last thing he needed was that final touch!

Fully intending to bid her good-night and take his leave, he found himself stepping up onto the porch. Without waiting for an invitation, he crossed to the swing where he had once spent many an hour weaving plots in his head—one or two of which he had since personally explored, a few of which he had only written about. "I'd better stay out here and drip awhile before I go next door, or I'll have that female dragon breathing fire down my neck. Is it men in general she hates, or is it just me?"

"Mrs. Mountjoy's not really a dragon. She's just got a lot on her mind lately, with the wedding and all. Charles's mother will be coming to help."

Kane nodded. Gently, he set the swing into motion. The summer night sounds, the smell of damp earth and newly cut grass, the squeak of the rusty old chain, all converged on him at once, bringing a fresh onslaught of memories. "I used to have a dog, back when I was in high school. Got her from the pound. Ginger, I called her."

Rory must have murmured something appropriate, because he went on as if she weren't even there. "I remember sneaking her upstairs nights after Mom went to sleep, and then, when she wanted to go out, I'd let her out the window onto the porch roof, and she'd climb down that trellis. Smartest dog in captivity."

"What happened to her?"

"Got hit by a truck the year after I went off to school."

And he had cried. Suddenly Rory knew it as well as she knew her own name. He would have been tall even then, and broad shouldered, with those same rugged masculine features, only slightly less well-defined, and he had cried his heart out over a mutt named Ginger from the pound. "I don't think there's much trellis left under all that wisteria," she said. "Charles wants me to cut it back. Maybe I'll do it tomorrow." Leaning back against the wall, she hooked her arms around her knee and stared at the dense, lacy vines. "He wanted to hire a man to root it out before it even bloomed."

"Too late. By now those roots cover half the county."

Rory nodded. After a while she said, "I wanted to do it with a justice of the peace. It would have been so much easier."

"Cut the wisteria with a J.P.?" Kane met her startled gaze and decided that her eyes were light brown. "Oh. Get married, you mean."

"Charles wants to do it in church. He says he owes it to me, since it's my first, but I'd just as soon not bother."

"To get married?" Kane's eyebrows, black and level, lifted again. His eyes were brown, the color of coffee with no cream.

"In a church. With all the people. And a rehearsal and everything, with dinner afterward. He's planning this big party after the wedding for all his business associates and clients."

Kane shrugged. Removing his shirt, he draped it over the back of the swing, and Rory carefully avoided looking directly at him. Nudity, even partial nudity, had always made her uncomfortable.

"You don't like parties?"

She sighed and twisted an end of hair around her finger. "It's not so much that, it's just—it's just *every-thing!*" She flung out both hands in a helpless gesture and then sighed again. "I'm sorry. You don't want to hear all this."

"No, that's all right. Sometimes it helps to dump on a stranger. Putting your problems into words might help you sort things out in your mind."

"I don't have any problems ... not real ones, anyway." She began punishing her hair again, twisting and

bending it, tugging it and brushing her cheek with the
soft curl on the end.

No, of course you don't, darling, Kane thought.
*That's why you're on your hands and knees scrubbing
the hell out of your front porch in the middle of the
night just two weeks before your wedding.*

For reasons he didn't even bother to try and understand, Kane began leading her skillfully with a few
seemingly innocent questions. Having been on the re-
ceiving end of more interviews than he could recall,
both as a writer and a decorated pilot, he was skilled at
the subtle, as well as the not-so-subtle techniques.

With Rory he was subtle. In no time at all he had her
pouring out all the things that had cluttered her mind
until sleep had been an impossibility.

"The thing is, I've always been so sensible—everybody says so—but lately, I just don't know what's
wrong with me. I can't make the smallest decision
without falling apart. Charles wanted me to decide last
week about flowers, and I keep putting it off. And then
there's the music. I can't decide between something
traditional or this old Janis Joplin record of my father's."

Kane mouthed a silent whistle. "You particularly
fond of the primal scream school of music?"

She shrugged. "I'm not musical at all. It was just
something Sunny suggested. She and Bill used to like
Joplin a lot."

"Sunny?"

"My mother. Her name was Margaret, but she had
it legally changed to Suriya, which means Sun. I think.
Anyway, everybody calls her Sunny."

Aurora, daughter of Suriya and God knows who.
Zeus? Zinna? Photinia? Things were finally beginning

to fall into place. The sixties syndrome strikes again. "Okay, if you don't have any particular choice, why not just ask the church musician to suggest something?"

"Well, yes…I suppose I could do that." She chewed on her lip until Kane was tempted to rescue it. "But I don't know who's supposed to pay for the music, or if they'll send a bill, or if you're supposed to slip them something in a sealed envelope. And besides, I didn't exactly agree to a church wedding, anyway."

"How about the church yard? The Bankses' backyard used to be pretty decent, for that matter. I got in after dark tonight, so I haven't seen it lately."

"Whatever." She sighed. "Anyway, Charles says I have to decide on all this junk pretty soon, and school starts in a month, and there's the dress, too."

"The dress. Right." Was money a problem? Kane wouldn't have thought so. Charles had majored in making a bundle at Carolina and dedicated himself to the process ever since, but she probably had too much pride not to want to do her part.

"I shouldn't make such a big deal of it. I mean, it's only for a few minutes, but—" She flung out her arms. "Oh, I don't know! I just can't seem to organize my mind! I used to be so good at it, but lately I can't seem to organize my own breakfast! I pour cereal into a bowl and then stare at it for half an hour, like I'm wondering what's supposed to happen next. I write all these notes to myself that don't make any sense when I read them again, and I make all sorts of lists and then forget where I put them."

Kane's gaze moved to her ankle, which couldn't have been any more perfect if it had been turned on a lathe. "Tie strings around your, er, finger, and then forget why?"

With an awkward grace that he found surprisingly touching, she twisted her ankle around and fingered the piece of dirty string there. "Oh. You mean this." He shrugged, not wanting to embarrass her. "It's for shoes."

"Seems logical enough to me."

"I don't think Charles would call it logical," she said morosely. "He'd probably call it stupid. But did you ever try to tie a string around your own finger? It's impossible. Besides, it gets in the way. This—" she touched her ankle "—was supposed to remind me to make up my mind whether or not I needed a new pair of shoes to be married in, and if I did, to get them in time to break them in so I won't end up limping up to the preacher with a blister on my heel."

"Did it work?"

"Sort of. At least I remembered what it was for," she said with a small, lopsided smile, which Kane found perilously close to irresistible.

He watched closely until the last glimmer of the smile had faded, almost wishing she hadn't done it. Or if she had, that he hadn't seen it. Damn! A single rueful little smile, along with the tousled hair and the wet, rumpled pajamas, gave her a dangerous kind of vulnerability— the kind he had always been a sucker for. He reminded himself that this was no ordinary woman. This was Charlie's plain, practical, sensible spinster school-teacher.

Jeez! *This* woman and Charles W. E. Banks III? She'd burn him alive! Even in kindergarten Charlie had been a bit of a stuffed shirt. Kane had dragged his chestnuts out of the fire more times than he could recall. Charlie would emerge from the fray without a hair out of place, while Kane, shorter and lighter, invariably came out bruised and bloodied, with his clothes in tatters.

And then he'd had to face his mother. He would rather have taken another licking than catch the razor-sharp edge of Sally Smith's tongue, God love her sweet soul. Funny how just seeing an old buddy could trigger an avalanche of memories.

"I know Charles is glad you're here."

He might be, Kane allowed... and then again, he might end up regretting his impulsive invitation. More likely, however, was that Kane would end up regretting it. "Look, I'd better let you get some sleep. I don't know what's on the slate for tomorrow, but—"

"Work. Charles is in the middle of a big settlement. He has to clear his desk before we go on our h-h-honeymoon."

H-h-honeymoon? It was a thoughtful man who sidled through the neatly pruned hedge just after one o'clock a.m. and let himself into the darkened house next door. A very thoughtful man.

Two

"Ta-dum-dum," Kane hummed absently. "For all-ll the wrong reasons."

"Don't tell me you're still harboring a secret desire to be a country-western star," said Charles, coming upon his friend sipping coffee and scanning the editorial page of the *Journal*.

Kane grinned up at the tall, blond man in the pale gray suit. On the hottest day of the year, Charlie Banks didn't sweat. There was something vaguely disturbing about that. "You'll notice the voice hasn't improved with age." Kane flexed his square-tipped fingers. "Remember that guitar I had back in junior high? Whatever happened to it?"

"If I'm not mistaken, you sat on it the night of the senior prom."

"Ouch," Kane winced. "It's beginning to come back to me now, and it's not a pretty picture. How did we ever survive, Charlie? Your car, my driving, your—"

"My boat at Lake Norman, your diving?"

"Waxing poetic on me? Is that what love does to men our age?"

"Not to me. I'm not the one reading George Wills and singing Earl Scruggs."

Tossing the paper aside, Kane chuckled. "Can't remember who recorded that particular number, but I'm pretty sure it wasn't Scruggs. What have you got lined up for today?"

"I'd like to take you over to meet Aurora. Then, if you don't mind, you could help with whatever needs doing. She's usually the soul of efficiency, but just lately she seems distracted."

Kane frowned. So what now? Did he confess that he had already met the woman, or did he shut up and let nature take its course? It occurred to Kane that if nature had truly taken its course, Charlie and Aurora Hubbard wouldn't even be friends, much less engaged to be married. A less likely pair he had yet to meet.

"I'm here to serve. But try to get off early, because frankly, man, I think you need to spend more time with your lady. Meanwhile, I'll mosey on over and introduce myself if you think it'll help."

"I'd appreciate that if you don't mind. If you could just urge her to get on with finalizing the plans, it would be a big help."

"Got it. Finalize plans, run any errands that need running, calm whatever nerves need calming, and if we hit a snag in the conversation, I can tell her all about your sordid past."

"What sordid past?" Charles exclaimed indignantly.

"Just joking," Kane reassured him. He'd forgotten his friend's lack of even a rudimentary sense of humor.

"Yes, well...just so you behave yourself with Aurora. She's not like the kind of women you always preferred."

"You ought to know, Charlie," Kane said softly, and then was sorry he had. Ancient history. Water over the dam. He had been dating Suzanne Goforth before Charlie had ever met her, and for a time the three of them had gone everywhere together. But in the end, Suzanne had chosen the business major with an established firm all ready to step into, over a wild-blue-yonder type who couldn't offer her much more than his name.

Rory woke up with a headache, which she put down to a weather front. Or possibly the fact that she had lain awake for hours after showering and going back to bed. Not even to herself would she admit it might have something to do with the fact that her feet were getting colder by the minute. In less than two weeks she'd be moving into the house next door, sharing a bed with Charles, sitting across the table from him every day. Did she love him enough for that?

Did she even know what love was? As a child she'd been taught that one loved one's fellow creatures—one's fellow animals, minerals and vegetables. The cosmic bouillabaisse called love united all creation in some sort of mystical brotherhood. Like the common cold virus, it was everywhere, inescapable, if not quite as unwelcome.

She'd always had trouble with the concept, especially as she grew older and began to see some of her fellow creatures a bit more clearly. Especially when a few of her fellow creatures had seen *her* more clearly and had liked what they'd seen.

With her grandmother, things had been simpler. There wasn't much talk about love, but there were rules one lived by. Obey the rules, and you were safe.

For a while after she'd gone out on her own, she'd been too busy making a place for herself to even think about love. Oh, sure, everyone still talked about it. They loved pizza, or Cajun music, or fried chicken. But people? One person in particular?

Rory loved her family. That was as far as she was willing to go with this universal love thing. She had never quite sorted it out in her mind. Oh, she'd had crushes, but as for anything more, she had taken the safest course and followed her grandmother's stern precepts. Those had clearcut boundaries. A respectable woman kept herself busy—the idle hands theory and all. She attended church regularly, tithed, filled her spare time with good works, didn't own a charge card, which was no more than the devil's calling card, and didn't wear dresses with necklines cut all the way down to her goozle and skirts cut all the way up to that same amorphous section of her anatomy.

Rory knew she was a good teacher. And while lately she'd been inclined to dither, at least her porch floor was clean, and so was her conscience. So maybe today she would tackle that wisteria she had promised to whack off. If she could find her whackers. The last time she'd used them had been to cut down an old clothesline in the backyard, and she had put them . . .

Shoving open the back door a few minutes later, she muttered, "Now let me see, if I were a pair of whackers, where would I be?"

Kane, his hand lifted to rap on her kitchen door, blinked. "At the Parawackers Paradise Motel and Chicken Delight?" he ventured.

After one stunned moment, Rory hooted. She laughed until tears spilled over her lashes and streaked down her cheeks. "No, but it sounds a lot more interesting than a garage shelf. Is there really such a place?"

"Probably not."

"Too bad," she said, grinning.

"If there were, would you meet me there for an illicit—"

"Chicken Delight? In a minute!" Rory was astonished at her instinctive response to this man. It wasn't like her at all.

Kane could think of a few other delights he'd rather explore, but those were not for him to discover. Would old Charlie recognize a genuine delight if he tripped over it? Probably not.

"I came to offer myself to you—at Charlie's suggestion. He's tied up at the office, but he hopes to be free this afternoon."

"Did you tell him about last night?"

"No. Should I have?"

"Well-ll . . . he might've misunderstood," Rory allowed.

Right. And a robin might eat worms. "So what's on the agenda? Picking out posies? Trying out wedding marches? Shopping for white satin slippers? Bundling up rice and rose petals into dainty little parcels?"

Rory's jaw fell. "Do I have to do that, too? Isn't it— uh—unenvironmental, or something like that?"

"Not as long as you don't cook it. What the birds don't eat will biodegrade. You might get picked up on a littering count, but with any luck, Charlie could get you off with a fine."

"Are you always so outrageous?"

"Only when I discover the perfect straight man," Kane replied solemnly. And then he grinned, his slightly crooked mouth twisting up at one corner in a way that Rory found totally captivating.

"I'm afraid I'm not very good at it. Being straight, that is. I mean playing straight man—woman!" By this time, Kane was laughing again, and Rory gave up and laughed with him. It was a remarkable experience. She felt as if she'd suddenly shed fifteen pounds.

"Today's agenda," she said when she'd sobered up, "includes pruning the wisteria and finding homes for my house plants. Charles doesn't care for house plants." And when Kane didn't react, she said, "Well, you did ask."

He glanced over her shoulder at the window shelf filled with leggy, moribund vegetables in Mason jars. "Right. Okay, first the wisteria . . . although I always kind of liked it shaggy. Makes a good cover for all sorts of skullduggery."

"According to Charles, it invites termites and dry rot."

"Charles is a Philistine."

"No, he's a Presbyterian. He started out a Baptist, but he switched," Rory said with a straight face, and then spoiled the effect by giggling. Giggling! She hadn't giggled in twenty years!

Kane located the pruning shears—the whackers—hanging among an array of dusty dried herbs Rory had plucked, bunched, hung and forgotten. "I was going to make gallons of fancy vinegars to give to my fellow teachers, but I never got around to it," she said, and Kane nodded. He was beginning to suspect the delightful Miss Aurora Hubbard never got around to a lot of worthwhile things. Charlie would soon change all that.

By noon the vine had been drastically cut back. Rory had winced with each snick of the blades. By the time it was done, she was close to tears. She said it looked awful, but Charles would probably approve.

As for Kane, he thought Rory looked delightful, freckled face, scratched arms, twiggy hair, mournful expression and all. Charlie would definitely disapprove—of her, at least. Which was a damned shame. Kane had enjoyed a lot of women once he had learned to appreciate what was inside a woman's head as much as what was inside her knickers. He couldn't remember one he had enjoyed more.

What the devil had made her settle for Charlie? Granted, he was a thoroughly decent guy—solvent, responsible, respectable. Not bad looking, either. Suzanne had chosen him over Kane, but dammit, Rory wasn't Suzanne! Underneath that prim, speckled facade, he'd caught too many glimpses of a funny, sexy, warm creature who bore no resemblance to the woman Charlie had described.

"How'd you two meet?" he asked as she poured two large glasses of some iced beverage that looked like pink lemonade that had gone slightly off.

"The house. I rented it from an agency. Charles came over to introduce himself the day I moved in and brought a set of instructions about garbage, utilities, maintenance and that sort of thing."

"Charlie would," said Kane after sipping the odd-tasting beverage. At least it was cold and wet, and his precious bodily fluids were in sore need of replenishing after a morning of sweaty whacker wielding.

"Well, yes...he's very conscientious," Rory said defensively.

"My thoughts, precisely. What is this stuff?" Kane held his empty glass aloft.

"Herbal tea. My father's in the business. Um—I think this one might be citrus-hibiscus. Mixed with some leftover flat diet cola."

"Sorry I asked."

"I should have offered you water. Not everyone likes herbal tea. At least not iced. At least not adulterated with poisonous chemicals. Bill—my father—doesn't believe in chemicals."

Kane let that one pass. "So what's next on the list?"

Rory glanced at the clock. It was 12:37, approximately twelve hours since she had first laid eyes on Kane Smith. It seemed more like twelve years. Or twelve lifetimes. "A bath, I guess."

Kane's brows lifted abruptly, and she grinned and waved a hand to erase her statement. "I don't need help with that one. If Charles comes home for lunch, though, I'd better be clean and dressed and have something fixed. You could stay," she added hopefully.

"Thanks, but I think I'll drive around, check out some of the old haunts. Maybe go into Winston and shop for a wedding gift."

"You don't have to—I mean, we don't expect—oh, Lordy, do what you want to, Kane. Charles said we have enough china from his first marriage, and he has the Banks silver—tons of the stuff. I don't know of anything we need, honestly." Kane watched, fascinated, as she nibbled on her full lower lip. He envied her teeth.

* * *

Half an hour later, driving south on Highway 52, he envisioned a glorious plaster of Paris Venus with a lamp for a head and a clock for a belly. And maybe a thermometer up her spine? He had a feeling Rory would love it. Charlie would hate it, but worse, he would be hurt and embarrassed, and feel that he had to apologize to his bride for his best friend's execrable taste.

Nah... it wasn't worth it. Maybe linens. Something tasteful and monogrammed, white on white.

And then he swore as his creative mind conjured up a vision of a naked and freckled Rory sprawled across white linen sheets with Charlie in his starched, striped, buttoned-up-to-the-chin pajamas.

This was crazy. By all rights Kane should be happy his friend had finally found a woman who stood a fair chance of breaking him out of his rigid shell. God knows, Kane had tried, but he'd been no match for Maddie Banks with her writ-in-stone rules of rectitude and her scorn for the lower classes—which definitely included the harried Sally Smith, waitress at a nearby country-food-and-music emporium, and her hell-raising son.

No, it was probably too late for poor old Charlie. Which was a damned shame, because there was a lot of good stuff there. Charlie was what was generally termed a sterling character.

But Charlie and Crystal Aurora Hubbard? She had inadvertently let slip her name last night, and Kane could tell she was embarrassed by it. Personally, he thought it delightful. He thought everything about the woman was delightful.

Which just might prove to be a problem.

Deliberately Kane directed his mind into safer channels: the work in progress, which he'd rough drafted before he'd taken off for Key West to gain some much-needed perspective on the plot. The pacing had been off, and he'd thought a change of scene might get his brain back on line.

Three days of soaking up salt-laden sunshine, a flaming fight with a flaming redhead, plus the binge that had followed his paying her off and putting her on a plane, hadn't done the trick.

Okay, so he'd been following a familiar pattern. Look for an attractive redhead, court her, win her and live happily ever after, with no more waking up alone, staring at the ceiling and wondering what was missing that made his successful life feel so damned empty.

He was getting too old for this particular drill. It never worked, anyway. None of the women, no matter how well they fit his physical specifications, seemed to fit his needs. Different values, different goals, which made real conversation impossible. They laughed at the wrong things, at the wrong times, or worse yet, didn't laugh at all. They moped when he wanted to be silent, wanted to dance when he was in the mood to talk, and when they did talk, it was always about themselves.

Hell, no wonder his pacing was off. He couldn't even pace his own life. He still hadn't figured out what was ailing his plot, and that had been the whole point of driving some fifteen hundred miles!

He gripped the wheel until his knuckles whitened, eyes narrowed against the midday glare. Then, out of nowhere came the echo of one of Rory's deadpan wisecracks, and he began to grin. *Ah, Charlie boy, you really hit the jackpot this time, you lucky son-of-a-gun!*

Homing in on the segment of plot that had bothered him for weeks, Kane let his intuition scan freely as he relaxed his grip on the steering wheel. Yeah. Okay. So what if he shifted the agent's entrance to the end of the ninth chapter instead of springing him in the seventh? What if he pulled the mole switch before the pipe bomb instead of afterward? What if—?

Right! Suddenly everything fell into place. No sag, no bag, no lost momentum. It was all in the timing.

Timing, he mused, picking up the what-if game he often played in his writing. What if he'd met Rory before Charlie had? What if he had come to visit Charlie and Suzanne, and Rory lived next door...

What, he wondered idly, had gone into making Rory Hubbard the unique creature she was? That quicksilver flash of wit that matched his own off-the-wall sense of humor, joke for joke. The warmth he sensed in her— the passion lying just beneath the surface, waiting to be lit. Who was she?

More to the point, what would the constant pressure of being Mrs. Charles William Edward Banks III do to her? One thing was pretty certain—she wouldn't be scrubbing any more porch floors after midnight. In her pajamas. Nor would she wear strings around her ankle to remind her to buy a new pair of shoes.

Where had she tied the string to remind her to buy the rest of her trousseau?

Marriage to Charlie, Kane thought rather sadly, was going to put a real damper on that delightful laughter of hers. Funny—it had never occurred to him that a woman's laughter could home in on a man's erogenous zones with such deadly accuracy.

Yeah ... it was a damned shame. About her sense of humor. About Charlie's lack of one. It occurred to

Kane that if a man were more of a friend—or possibly less of one—he might just be tempted to save those two from ruining each other's lives.

Rory was invited to dinner with Charles and Kane at the big house that night. And that was another thing, she reminded herself as she tilted her head before the mirror to put on her small pearl earrings—she was going to have to remember not to call Charles's house the big house. It sounded too much like a prison.

It was big, though. Big, square and uncompromising, it reminded her, entirely too much for comfort, of Charles's mother. Rory had met Madeline Banks only briefly, the first year she had moved to Tobaccoville. Suzanne had been living next door then, and although Rory had liked Suzanne, she'd never really known her well. Charles's first wife hadn't been the neighborly sort. Evidently, she slept most of the morning and went out in the afternoons. Now and then, with the windows open, Rory had been embarrassed to hear her arguing with someone—either Charles or Mrs. Mountjoy. Suzanne had had the kind of voice that carried. An uncharitable person might have called it shrill.

Rory wasn't particularly looking forward to meeting Madeline Banks again. Still less was she looking forward to the inevitable meeting of Bankses and Hubbards en masse. Maybe her family wouldn't be able to come, after all. Or maybe Mrs. Banks would be tied up with her daughter, who, according to Charles, was in the throes of her second divorce.

Sighing, Rory smoothed her hair, which she had arranged the way Charles liked it, in a neat vertical roll at the back of her head. She dusted a layer of powder over her face, for all the good it would do, and applied a faint hint of coral to her lips with the tip of her little finger. A final pat to the lacy-edged collar of her white lawn blouse, and she slipped into the jacket of her pale gray linen suit—her PTA suit. She had bought it the year she had first begun teaching at Old Richmond Elementary School, a few miles down the Tobaccoville Road.

Mrs. Mountjoy's cooking was up to her usual standards, which evidently suited Charles just fine. The cream-of-library-paste soup was followed by a serving of petrified chicken, overcooked asparagus, watery applesauce, and bits of cabbage afloat in a sea of mayonnaise, which Rory assumed was supposed to be cole slaw.

Charles sat at one end of the massive oval table, with Rory at the other end and Kane halfway between the two of them. Once they were married, she might suggest they remove a few of the leaves unless there were guests.

Rory helped herself to rolls and offered the basket first to Kane and then to Charles, who was describing in great detail a case he was currently working on. Rory stifled a yawn. Her eyes strayed to Kane, and she caught a look of—of what? Commiseration?

Abruptly, she sat up straighter and pinned a smile on her face as Charles droned on and on. Rory wasn't musical. Liked it, but just couldn't *do* it. But even she could recognize the need for an occasional change of pitch.

"Maryland," Kane said suddenly, picking a single word from the monologue. "Hey, do you remember that weekend we drove up the Eastern Shore with these two girls from—"

"Yes, well—I'm sure Aurora doesn't want to hear about our youthful follies. As I was saying, the state of Maryland has this provision in the—"

Aurora decided she would very much like to hear about their youthful follies. Not that she believed Charles had actually had any. Or participated in any. Or been subjected to any.

"Do you *do* a folly, or is it done to you?" she mused. "Or is it one of those little architectural do-hickies people put in their backyards? No, that's a gazebo, isn't it?" Suddenly she became aware that she had spoken aloud and that both men were staring at her. "I'm sorry," she said, flushing. "Please, go on with what you were saying, Charles, I'm sure it's fascinating."

And Charles did. Endlessly. While Kane covered his twitching lips with his napkin.

Oh, God, she couldn't go through with it. All her life she had thought of middle-class respectability as a sort of Holy Grail. All she had ever wanted in life was to marry some suit-wearing, briefcase-carrying business man and have her two-point-whatever children in a regular hospital, and name them Sam or John or Betty Jane or Mary Ann.

Her three younger sisters, Glorious Peace, Fauna Love and Misty Morn, had never seemed to mind living in a compound with thirty-seven other people, where the air was thick with smoke—campfire and otherwise—where there was no discipline, no rules and no privacy, where family meant the entire group instead of a man and a woman and their children. A place where no one went to church, but where grown men sat cross-legged in diapers and stared at the sky for hours and women chanted and danced in circles around trees. Where weeds were eaten, smoked and worshiped, and children were given beads and scarves to play with instead of dolls and guns so that their tender little minds would not be warped with false role models or notions of war.

Rory loved her parents, she really did, but she had sometimes resented them. She loved her sisters, having watched them all enter the world. To her way of thinking, birth was a miserable spectator sport. It was messy and noisy and scary as the devil to a child of three, despite the fact that each birth was accompanied by original music from different members of the community and that her mother, between panting, grunting and groaning, had recited verses written especially for each child.

Rory would have preferred watching cartoons, not that anyone in the commune would have been caught dead owning a television set. She would have preferred going to school and Sunday school and Fourth of July parades wearing ordinary dresses or jeans, instead of going to sit-ins and protest marches wearing her father's tie-dyed T-shirts.

Rory had been eleven when the Hubbards had suddenly picked up and left the commune, which by then had dwindled to less than two dozen members, some said because an injunction had been taken out against them by the department of sanitation, others said because the landowner they leased from had been offered a fortune from a developer and was buying his way out of the lease.

Whatever the reason, she had been relieved when she'd been sent to live with her grandmother until the Hubbards could find another place to settle. The younger children had stayed with their parents, but Rory, enrolled in a real school for the first time, had stayed on with her grandmother in Kentucky. After a while, Bill and Sunny had settled in Virginia, and Bill had turned his interest in herbs into a surprisingly successful business. Eventually they had become, somewhat to their own surprise—capitalists!

Rory was the only one of the four girls who had gone to college. She'd felt guilty when her grandmother had left her the money, but that hadn't stopped her. Sunny had wanted her to study folklore, music and art. Bill had suggested a major in horticulture with a minor in business, but by then Rory had known what she wanted to be.

A schoolteacher. It might not be the most exciting career in the world, but it was respectable and unremarkable, and she had never once regretted it.

Although just lately she had begun to wonder if it had been the right choice. Something was definitely ailing her lately, and she couldn't think of anything else it might be.

"Aurora, would you care for more coffee with your cake?"

Rory blinked away the past and cautiously poked a fork at the slab of dry pound cake the housekeeper had placed before her. "Coffee would be nice," she told Charles.

All right, so she liked coffee. Did that make her a traitor? Hubbard's Heavenly Herbals was hardly going to go belly-up just because one member of the family occasionally drank something besides Chamomile Comfort.

Besides, it was time she realigned her loyalties. In a few days she would no longer be a Hubbard, she would be Mrs. C. W. E. Banks III. Charles looked on herbs as vaguely subversive, if not downright illegal—although he didn't mind mint jelly with his lamb or sage in his country sausage.

Maybe next year she'd try him with the vinegars.

And then Kane asked about Charles's family, and Rory was off the hook again, free to let her mind roam. Was it her fault if it kept roaming back to Charles's best man? Her grandmother had taught her all she needed to know about physical discipline, but she'd never discussed the need for mental discipline. Still, after four years of college and four years of teaching, one would've thought she would have had her mind under better control.

And as if the daydreams weren't bad enough, last night she had dreamed something she didn't even know *how* to dream! She had woken up tingling all over, her pajamas drenched with sweat and her heart racing like a jackhammer.

Rory peered at her fiancé, wishing she could blame it on him. Women in love were supposed to daydream, weren't they? Charles was handsome enough to figure in any woman's dreams.

The trouble was, the man in her dream had not been Charles.

Charles stood and led them into the front parlor so that Mrs. Mountjoy could clear the table. "'Wall Street Week' is on in five minutes," he said, and Rory hid her disappointment. She had hoped they might have some time together to relax, maybe even to cuddle a bit. Sooner or later she was going to have to prepare herself for—for *it*.

"I think I'll go out on the porch and sit awhile," Kane said.

Wistfully, Rory watched him go. She liked the way he moved, as if he were a piece of powerful, well-oiled machinery. Then the screen door closed behind him, and resigned to a dull evening, she took her place beside Charles on the maroon damask chesterfield.

Maybe Ruykyser would be funny tonight, she thought hopefully. His dreadful puns flew right over Charles's head, but Rory enjoyed them. Which was only fair, she told herself. If she had to sit through Charles's business shows for the next fifty years, she deserved some reward.

At nine sharp Charles switched off the set and turned to her on the sofa. Rory took a deep breath and focused her eyes on his mouth, which was really a very nice mouth. Not too full, not too thin. Not at all lopsided, like some mouths were....

"Did I tell you my mother will be coming sometime next week? She's invited my sister along. You haven't met Eve, but I believe you two will get along just fine. Eve can help you shop for any last-minute odds and ends you still need to buy."

Last-minute odds and ends? She hadn't even decided on a wedding dress yet, much less bought one. The list headed "Trousseau" contained exactly two items: bathrobe and raincoat.

"That sounds lovely," she said, cold perspiration filming her forehead.

"I'm afraid I'll be even busier than usual right up until the wedding, my dear." Covering her hand with his, Charles smiled, and Rory smiled bravely back. His teeth were an orthodontist's dream. Good prenatal nutrition, no doubt. Did an early diet of bean curd and wild greens produce good bones and teeth? she wondered absently.

"But at least," Charles went on, "we'll be able to get away afterward for a few days. I've already made our

reservations in Cincinnati. We'll have a suite, all to
ourselves.'' He beamed, and Rory tried to look appro-
priately thrilled. Cincinnati might not be every woman's dream of a honeymoon destination, but when there
was a convention of certified life underwriters there at
the same time, it would be foolish not to take advantage of it.

"I understand, Charles. I'm busy, too, what with
getting the house ready to move over here and trying to
get a head start on some of my classroom projects for
this fall. In fact, I was going to dye some beeswax tonight. I left it melting over a slow burner while I—''

"You left something cooking?" Charles frowned.

"On low heat. Barely up to a simmer. It's a big pot,
honestly, and there's not a chance—''

"There's always a chance, Aurora," Charles said
impatiently.

"Always a chance for what?" drawled Kane, the
screen door punctuating his words.

"I'll be back shortly, Kane. Aurora left the stove on."
Charles grabbed her by the hand and practically
dragged her out of the room, and Rory sent Kane a de-
spairing, embarrassed look over her shoulder.

Hell and damnation. What was wrong with those
two? Charlie treated her as if she were a piece of office
furniture, and that was when he wasn't treating her like
a misbehaving child.

What the devil did she see in him, anyway? Was she
attracted to his bank account? Kane could have told her
that Charlie would have everything sewn up in gilt-
edged securities and annuities, tighter than a tick on a
short-haired dog.

No, dammit, it wasn't the money! Kane didn't know
what it was, but he knew her better than that. He knew,

too, after less than twenty-four hours, that Charlie was going to strangle everything that was sweet and gentle and funny and spontaneous in Rory Hubbard.

God alone knew what she would do to him. Wring him dry as a gourd in bed. Under all that funny earnestness, that flaky sense of humor, there was one thoroughly sexy lady, just waiting to have her fuse lit, and Kane was beginning to wonder if Charlie was capable of lighting it. He was becoming more certain by the minute that it hadn't happened yet. And that, for some reason, gave him an inordinate sense of relief.

"Oh, hell," Kane muttered in disgust. If he didn't watch it, he might just wind up writing romances instead of thrillers! The sooner he put a wrap on this wedding thing and got back to the underground resurgence of the KGB, the better for all concerned.

Three

___

While Charles dealt with the whimsies of a certain inspector who found it necessary to make a dozen trips to the beach to appraise a single cottage, Kane set himself out to be obliging to the bride-to-be. She was evidently under a good deal of stress, and Kane had had some experience with that condition.

"First off, I suggest we find those lists of yours and get started on what needs finishing up. Zero hour is eleven days and counting."

Rory dropped onto a kitchen chair and raked her green-dyed fingers through her hair. "Don't remind me," she groaned, which Kane considered a curious response for a woman about to be married to the man of her choice. "I've lost my notes. I never lose things, but—"

"Never mind, I'm a whiz at rounding up stray notes. I've outlined entire books on the backs of envelopes, napkins and match covers and lived to tell the tale. Literally. God, I'm getting in deeper by the moment, aren't I?''

Rory laughed, but it was a weak effort. She'd had another restless night. It was getting to be a habit. "That's right, you're a writer, aren't you? Charles said you'd had something published. That's nice.''

Kane absorbed the blow to his ego without a whimper. Actually, it was kind of refreshing. But then, coming from Aurora, a kick in the butt might be refreshing. If he didn't watch it, he was going to find himself dangerously besotted by the woman.

"Thank you," Kane said. "Now, if you'll point me in the general direction, I'll go bird-dog your lists.''

Rory closed her eyes. Ten seconds later she said, "Look under the top catalog on the bottom bookshelf. If they're not there, look under the telephone. Oh, and you might try the bathroom footstool.''

Kane nodded. "Pretty much where I figured they'd be. Need any help cleaning up that mess on your hands? What is it, by the way?''

"It's beeswax. For modeling. For my children.''

Eyes twinkling, he said gravely, "Right. You and Charlie are going to experiment with a new style of procreation.''

"Not *my* children—my *children!* My students, that is. It's sort of like modeling clay, only it smells better and doesn't crumble. Actually, I use it as a lead-in for an elementary biology lesson.''

"Birds and bees?''

Rory sent him a quelling look, and then she grinned. "Bees and flowers. We don't add birds to the mixture until third grade.''

Kane went off in search of her elusive lists, and while she deliberated how to get the wax film out of her stainless-steel stock pot, Rory continued to wonder about him. Charles had said the two of them had grown up together, and that Kane was some sort of writer, and Rory had drawn on her limited experience with the breed. Never in a million years could she have imagined someone like Kane Smith. As a child she had known a few poets. In college she'd come across a few academic writers, not a one of whom bore the least resemblance to Charles's writer friend. Kane was so— He was just so—

All right, she told herself as she ran scalding water into the pot and closed her mind to what was happening in the grease trap below—so he's sexy and good-looking and fascinating, and easy to talk to. So were half a million other men, no doubt. At least Kane, unlike a few of the more literary types she had met, seemed to have both feet planted firmly in the real world.

Of course, he was no Charles Banks. Charles was a certified life underwriter, head of the agency his father had founded. He was a serious, hard-working, successful businessman, highly respected in the community; a contributor to every legitimate charity, a gentleman her grandmother would have heartily approved of.

Rory grimaced as she caught sight of her viridian fingernails. Dishwashing detergent hadn't quite done the job. Charles's nails were always flawlessly manicured, she thought guiltily.

"Face it," she muttered. "Clean fingernails and all, Charles is about as exciting as a mashed-potato sandwich."

"What d'you say?" Kane called from the front room.

"Nothing!" Rory yelled back, appalled at the direction her thoughts had been taking all too frequently of late. It was sheer bridal nerves. It had to be. Otherwise, nothing made any sense. Charles was everything she had ever wanted in a husband...wasn't he? Her grandmother had told her too many times what happened to foolish girls who left home to follow the first good-looking bounder who passed their way.

"I've rounded up a few lists, but I don't think I've found 'em all," Kane said from the doorway. He was clutching a fistful of notes, scribbled on scratch paper, cash register tapes and the backs of envelopes. Rory was an inveterate list maker. It was a part of her organized personality.

"Shall we start with the top of the pile?" Kane, his face suspiciously solemn, read off two items. "Ants and dishwater."

"Oh." Her grandmother had once told her that dishwater would keep ants off the chrysanthemums. Rory had tried it and discovered that while her grandmother's Octagon soap might have worked wonders, her own ants thrived on liquid detergent. "Never mind that one, go on to the next one. Or better yet, let me have them." Rory had her own brand of shorthand. Besides, she had just remembered a note she'd just as soon not have to explain.

Scanning the first few lists, she muttered under her breath, "Done. Done." And then, "Oops, too late." And then, "Maybe..." The next one, she crumpled quickly and tossed into the garbage can.

One look at her flaming face and Kane would have given a year's royalties to know what was on it. It had looked like the one that had read, "Call gyno for appt!!!"

Birth control? To be sure they had sorted all that business out long before now. Unless . . .

"Honey, you're not pregnant, are you? Is that what's been bugging you?" The flush faded, leaving her pale between her freckles. Her eyes were enormous. If it weren't so crazy, Kane would have said she looked scared to death. "Rory? Baby, what's wrong? You can tell me—that's what best men are for, didn't you know? We're guaranteed to know all the answers."

This was one problem that answers alone couldn't solve, but Rory could hardly tell him that. She couldn't tell him anything, because there was only one way to solve this particular problem, and she had already put it off far too long. About ten years too long. "Let me clean this gunk off my hands, and I'll make us some tea and we can go out on the front porch."

Kane studied her pale speckled face, the shadowed amber eyes, the drooping mouth. She hadn't denied it, but neither had she admitted it. Neither a yes nor a no, not even a maybe.

Not even a maidenly "How-dare-you, sir!"

Reluctantly he gave up the idea of hauling her into his arms and holding her there until laughter chased the shadows from her eyes and passion darkened them. "Give me those lists," he said gruffly. "Time's wasting. We're going to have to get moving on some of this stuff, you know." He glanced down and then up again, frowning. "Wedding dress? You mean you really haven't even thought about it?"

Rory reached for one of the tin canisters that held her father's product. He sent it to her in bulk—the whole family served as unofficial taste testers. She was never quite sure what she was drinking, but most of it was at least passable. At any rate, it was probably healthy.

Having spent the first eleven years of her life eating nuts, berries, leaves, grains, sprouts and tofu, she had spent the last part of it satisfying her body's natural craving for junk food.

While they sipped iced glasses of something bland and yellowish that might or might not have been lemon grass, Rory explained about the dress. "The thing is, until we decide where we're going to be married, I won't know what kind of a dress I'll need. Charles used to belong to Macedonia Baptist. I go to first one church and then another, but I never got around to moving my membership from Grandma's church near Lexington, Kentucky. I'd really rather not bother with anything fussy, but Charles said his mother would probably have a few ideas."

Knowing Madeline Banks, Kane would swear to it. However, waiting until a few days before the ceremony to decide where it would be held was skating too close for comfort, even for an ex-chopper jockey with a high tolerance for adrenaline. "And what about Miss Aurora? Given a choice, what would she choose?"

"Kane, some days I can't even make up my mind which end of my toothbrush to squirt the toothpaste on, much less decide where I want to be married. I think it must be mental fatigue—I remember reading this article... Or was that metal fatigue?"

"I dunno. Are you showing any signs of cracks in your fuselage?"

"No, but I ran out of blueberry syrup last night and cried for twenty minutes, and I don't even *like* blueberry syrup! And that's just not like me! I've never been the emotional type." She sighed. "Why can't Charles just make an appointment with a preacher somewhere

and tell me when and where to show up? Is that too
much to ask?''

"Honey, you're supposed to be a part of the deci-
sion-making process. It's not like you were deciding
where to get your brakes relined. This is supposed to be
a momentous occasion in a woman's life. Charlie said
you'd never been married before.''

She nodded morosely. After noisily sucking up the
last of her tea through the ice cubes, she set the glass on
the railing and shoved the swing into motion. Smoothly
Kane adapted to the rhythm and they swung lazily for
several moments. Then Rory jammed both feet flat on
the floor, causing the swing to jerk back and forth until Kane brought it under control.

He turned to her and waited, noting the jut of her
chin, the militant spark in her large, shadowed eyes.
Obviously she had reached a decision. About something, anyway.

"All right! Today, I'll pick out a blasted dress!''

"That's flinging down the gauntlet, all right,'' he said
mildly. "You want to tackle it on your own, or do you
need moral support?''

She looked at him, and Kane could have wished he
weren't quite so aware of the silken texture of her skin.
She was a study in monochrome, from her topaz eyes to
her amber freckles, to her sun-streaked hair. She
smelled faintly of spice, faintly of beeswax, and wholly
delicious, and it occurred to him that if he knew what
was good for him, he would get the hell out of town before he did something dastardly. It wasn't as if he and
Charlie were all that close anymore. Suzanne notwith-
standing, there were some things a guy just didn't do,
not if he wanted to live with himself.

Rory sighed. "I ought to go by myself, but I'd probably end up going to a movie instead and then eating a whole box of Popsicles out of sheer guilt. I don't know what's happened to me lately, I really don't! I'm not at all this way."

"Is that a yes, you want me, or a no, you don't need me?"

She clutched his arm. "Please! I want you, I need you, only you've probably got lots more interesting things to do."

Kane could think of a few dozen more interesting things to do. Unfortunately, they all involved Aurora Hubbard.

Rory called Charles's office and left word that as long as they'd be in town shopping, why didn't the three of them have lunch together before driving back out to Tobaccoville? "I'll check again after we get done," she told the superefficient Mrs. Spainhour.

Shopping with Kane was an experience. The man was tricky! First, he made her decide what kind of dress she wanted—white satin with a train? Pink and long, with ruffles and lace? Something about midthigh length in red velvet?

"Velvet for this time of year?" she crowed. "Besides, I can't wear short skirts, my knees are too knobby."

"Just narrowing down the choices. What about something street length in honey tones?"

"You mean brown?"

"Did I say brown?"

"Honey's brown."

"I'm talking sourwood, not buckwheat," he said, and she laughed.

Really, shopping could be fun with the right companion. Why hadn't she thought of that before? Possibly because she had never before found just the right companion, Rory told herself, and quickly pushed the thought away.

They settled on a dressy suit in a pale tea-colored silk jacquard, and Rory tried not to flinch at the price tag. It wasn't every day a woman got married. She could afford, for once in her life, to splurge.

After that, there were shoes to buy, and Kane dismissed the salesman and seated himself on the fitting stool, sliding her right foot in and out of shoe after shoe, which the clerk brought out from the stockroom at Kane's request. Some were pretty, but miserable. Some were ugly, but comfortable. Kane insisted on buying her a pair of lacy, sequin-covered sneakers because she said they were totally impractical, and she *never* did anything impractical.

Finally they selected a pair of coffee-colored silk pumps as the perfect accessory for her suit. By that time Rory was weak from laughter and tingling from the soles of her feet all the way up just from the touch of Kane's hands. *All* the way up!

"I'd better call Charles," she said a bit breathlessly as they passed a row of pay phones. "He's probably wondering where we are." And while Kane pretended to stagger under the suit box, the two shoe boxes and a hatbox containing a confection of pearls, beige velvet leaves and veiling that Kane had insisted on buying for her, Rory dialed the pay phone.

"The Banks Agency," Charles's secretary announced.

"Mrs. Spainhour, is Charles tied up? This is Aurora. Hubbard. Charles's fiancée, that is." Oh, for heaven's sake, if Charles's secretary didn't know who Aurora Hubbard was by now, she probably never would! And what difference did it make, anyway? Soon she would be Aurora Banks.

"Mr. Banks left a message for you, Miss Hubbard. His mother has arrived, and he's gone home. You and Mr. Smith are to have lunch with them at Mr. Banks's house."

Rory hung up the phone slowly, all the joy having gone out of the morning. She felt as if someone had placed a heavy horse collar around her shoulders. "We're to go back home and have lunch with Charles and his mother."

"Oh."

Oh, indeed, Rory though twenty minutes later as they sped north on Highway 52. She had almost suggested they take the long way home, but Kane might have misunderstood. He might have thought she was not looking forward to her second meeting with the woman who would soon be her mother-in-law.

He would have been right.

"Where are you going?" Kane asked. He was driving. He enjoyed driving. Rory didn't. Besides, her car was a mess.

"Why—home, I thought. I'll just dash in and put my new things away and then go on over. Charles hates unpunctuality."

"No, I meant for your honeymoon."

"My h-h-honeym-m-m— The wedding trip?"

Kane slanted her a searching look. "It's a part of the usual package deal. Wedding. Wedding trip. Niagara Falls? Surely Charles didn't leave that decision for you, too?"

"Oh, no. That is, there's this underwriters' convention in Cincinnati, and Charles thought—that is, he's booked us a suite in the same hotel for the four-day weekend."

Charlie, you cork-brained jackass, you didn't! "Wasn't there someplace you'd rather go? Hawaii? The Caribbean? Alaska? Death Valley?"

Rory's weak smile flickered and was gone so quickly Kane almost missed it. Something was wrong here. Something was definitely wrong. He could leave now, before he brought the whole flaming mess down around their heads, or he could try to set things straight between these two. If it was possible to set things straight between two such dissimilar people.

"Okay, that's two things out of the way. Wedding outfit and honeymoon. And Madeline's going to decide where to hold the festivities, right?" Kane felt like slamming his fist into something hard, which wasn't going to solve a damned thing.

What the hell was wrong with the woman? She wasn't a wimp! She might act like one, but he'd seen through that act right off. So why was she meekly going along with this damned charade?

It's none of your business, man. She's nothing to you! And whatever friendship you and Charlie shared ended years ago. You don't owe him a damned thing, especially not after he stole your woman!

Kane tried and failed to work up his anger over the girl he had loved and lost a dozen or so years ago. Other than her red hair and a habit of giggling, he could barely remember her now. But *this* woman—this Crystal Aurora creature—! He could chart every freckle on her sweet, funny face with his eyes closed! It didn't make any sense.

Downshifting, he passed a moving van, driving with the skill of a man used to being in control. "So what's next on the agenda? What about your attendants? Have you decided who, how many and what they'll wear?"

Rory whimpered and dug out her handkerchief to wipe her damp forehead.

"Charles has a sister," Kane said, cutting her a sharp look of concern. "Eve used to be a pretty decent sort, not that I knew her all that well. She had her sights set a lot higher than the Smith kid next door." He chuckled. And then he glanced across the console and swiftly pulled over into the trouble lane, switching off the engine.

Kane had seen panic before. Gently, he pried Rory's icy fingers apart and cupped them between his own hands. "Honey, look at me. Breathe, dammit! No, not like that! Ah, hell, baby, what's wrong? Nothing can be that bad." He gathered her in his arms and unconsciously began kneading the rigid tendons at the back of her neck. "Was it something I said? Then consider it unsaid. If you're afraid Eve's going to barge in at the last minute and start throwing her weight around, forget it. It's your wedding—you can have it any way you want."

"It's not going to work, is it?" she asked in a bleak little voice.

Kane slipped his fingers up under her hair and stroked her nape. What could he say? She was dead right. A good marriage between those two had about as much chance of happening as a big tax cut. "You want me to talk to Charlie for you? Is that it?"

She leaned back against his arms, and he was relieved to see that some of the color had returned to her face. "Charles can't decide. He doesn't even know them.'' And then she shuddered, and Kane wondered just when he had stepped over into the twilight zone.

"Know who, Rory? Who is it that Charles doesn't know?"

"My sisters,'' she whispered. "My family. Kane, he'll hate them, and they'll laugh at him, and it will be awful!''

Kane swallowed a niggling feeling of disappointment. "I gather you have more than one sister, right? And you're not sure Charles will—ah—take to them?''

Wordlessly, Rory nodded. She could see it now. They would drive up in that awful van, with the big rainbow painted on the side and Hubbard's Heavenly Herbals in grass green letters four feet high. Sunny would be wearing one of her original creations and Bill would be—well, sartorially speaking, the good Lord only knew what stage he was in now. The last time she had been home, his favorite "business suit'' had been a double-breasted, bell-bottomed brown thing with mustard pinstripes he had picked up at a flea market. By now he might have graduated to white tie and tails. Or top hat and toga. With Bill, there was no predicting.

"Are your sister's going to stand up with you? How many are there, by the way?''

"Three,'' Rory said hopelessly. "Fauna, Misty and Peace. Peace is the oldest after me. Misty's the baby.''

"She might do as a flower girl,'' Kane responded and then wondered why she suddenly began to laugh.

"Oh, they'd all do wonderfully well as flower girls. Especially Sunny.''

"Your mother?''

She nodded. "Kane, I may as well warn you, I came from a family of flower children who never quite made it into the real world. Oh, well—I guess Peace did. She's on her second divorce, and to tell you the truth, I'm not sure even now that Bill and Sunny were ever legally married. I never dared ask, and Grandma said . . ."

All of which was pretty much what Kane had figured. A refugee from the golden age of idealism that was going to spread peace and harmony and love among all mankind.

"Honey, if that's all that's worrying you, forget it. Charlie and I didn't spring full grown out of the nineties, you know. I promise you, we can handle it."

And then, knowing he was probably making the worst mistake of his entire life, Kane went ahead and made it anyway. He kissed her. It was meant to be a gentle, reassuring kind of kiss, he told himself, knowing at the time he was lying.

He didn't want to reassure her. What he wanted was to drive her right out of Charlie's arms and into his own, and if that made him a son of a bitch, so be it.

Breaking away with the trembling softness of her lips indelibly impressed on his consciousness, Kane struggled to regulate his breathing—not to mention a few other bodily functions that had slammed instantly into condition red. He stared at her for one blinding moment, and then he shook his head as if to clear it.

"Like I said—don't worry about your family. We can handle it," he said hoarsely.

Sure, he could. He'd served on three continents, in one invasion and one war. He had handled that all right, hadn't he? He had walked away from a crash with nothing more than a bad back, dealt with a marriage that had begun to disintegrate almost before the ink was dry on the certificate, dealt with a little laser surgery on his eyes.

The thing was, he wondered as he drove them home to lunch with Maddie Banks and her favorite chick—could he handle watching Rory give herself to Charlie Banks?

Because God help him, all in the world he wanted to do right now was to take Charlie's lady into that shabby little bungalow, lower her onto the nearest bed, and find out for himself if she was covered all over with freckles.

And if she was, he wanted to taste every single one of them, to kiss every single one, and then to start all over again. And if that turned him into a frog, so be it. He would deserve it. But God! It would be worth it!

It wasn't as bad as Rory had anticipated. It was worse. She looked to Kane, instinctively seeking support, and he winked at her reassuringly. Madeline Banks had obviously set herself out to be charming, and when that happened, Kane knew from past experience it was time to stand by to take on casualties.

Nor were they long in coming. "Kane, how nice to see you. I hope your mother is well?"

Rory sent Kane a stricken look. She knew for a fact that his mother had died fairly recently after a lingering, painful illness. That first night, when he had found her scrubbing the front porch, they had both talked with an unexpected openness.

She needn't have worried. Mrs. Banks didn't expect a response. "Charles, this house should have been painted last year. How many times must I remind you? Every six years without fail. Your father and I made it a policy, and we never had cause to regret it."

"Mother, I—"

"Have you had the wiring inspected lately? I noticed an extension cord in the front parlor. Your father would never have one of those things in the house, and—"

"But, Mother—"

"In our business, we can't afford to be careless. It's up to us to set an example. Your father always said—"

"Mother, this house was wired before television sets were even thought of. And it's not like a single exten—"

"Miss Hubbard, I don't believe we've met before." Madeline tilted her head for a closer examination, and it occurred to Rory that if the woman could put her under a microscope, she would.

"I believe we were introduced soon after I—"

"Who are your people? I don't believe I know any Hubbards."

"Well, um—maybe you've heard of—"

"Aurora is not from around here, Mother," Charles put in.

At Rory's miserable look, Kane felt a further softening of an organ he could have sworn had long since been permanently hardened. Dammit, why didn't Charlie stand up for the woman he was planning to marry? Madeline would scare hell out of Dracula! Kane didn't care for his own sake. The woman had long since placed him off the lower end of her personal social scale and was perfectly capable of overlooking his existence, as long as he no longer attempted to lead her precious Charles astray.

But Rory was another matter. Damned if he'd stand by and watch the old battle-ax crush her into the ground.

"Miss Hubbard's family will be arriving in plenty of time for the ceremony," he said when no one else seemed anxious to reply.

"Mmm, yes. Well, I suppose that's only to be expected. Where do you propose to put them up, dear?" Before Rory could answer, she went on to say, "I know good and well you don't have room in that cramped little cottage. I begged Elton to tear it down so we could extend the lawn, but he thought we might need it someday, as a sort of dower cottage, you understand. Although how he thought I could live and breathe in such cramped quarters, I'll never know."

"Mother, I told Aurora her family could—"

"Of course, the closest decent hotel is in Winston. It's inconvenient, but then, I suppose they'll only be here for a day or so. How many of them are there?" she asked and rushed on to add, "Not too many, I hope. I hate to have the lawn trampled. My grass is in bad enough shape as it is. Oh, well, we'll just have to keep it small. My roses aren't up to par this year, anyway. Charles, how many times do I have to remind you that the air has to circulate. You've let the azaleas get leggy, to, and I know good and well the lilies haven't been divided in years. You promised me faithfully you would—"

Kane was staring fixedly at a spot on the wall. Rory stared at it, too. By the time coffee was served, her tongue had been bitten so many times it was probably bleeding. Her ears would be ringing for days.

Eleven days, she thought. Eleven days and it would all be over, and with any luck, they wouldn't be subjected to another visit for at least a year. And if Charles dared to say one word to her about her own family, she would crown him with his grandmother's precious Georgian silver coffeepot!

"Cream, Aurora?" Madeline Banks offered.

"Oh. Yes, please!" Startled, Rory shoved her freshly filled cup across the table, sloshing coffee all over the heirloom rice-linen cloth. Closing her eyes, she prayed for instant invisibility, and barring that, for a lapse of consciousness that would carry her through the next two weeks.

Make that three weeks. Better yet, three years! "Charles," she murmured, bracing herself to make an escape. "Would you mind if I—"

"I've decided to have the reception at the club. Eve will be here tomorrow, so she can take charge of that, although I must say, Aurora, you've left it shamefully late. They'll just have to squeeze us in the best way they can—after all, the Banks name should stand for something in this community. Charles, is Modene still organist at the church? I'll want her to play for the wedding, but I don't believe we'll need a soloist, under the circumstances. After all, it's not as though this is your first wedding."

Rory told herself that she'd got her wish. She hadn't wanted to have to make any decisions concerning the occasion, and now she didn't have to. It was all being taken out of her hands. So why did it rankle so?

When there was a pause in Madeline Banks's monologue, Rory got to her feet and carefully placed her translucent china cup on the table, embarrassed all over again by the coffee-stained cloth. "I'm afraid I'll have to go," she murmured, glancing expectantly at her fiancé.

"Charles," his mother said, "you'll remember I wrote you my lease is running out in September? I've

had some grave doubts about renewing it. I am seriously considering—'' She broke off with a pointed look
at Kane. ''My dear, would you mind seeing Miss—um,
Hubbard home? It's been so lovely, Aurora. I'm sure
we'll be seeing lots of each other from now on, but you
do look exhausted. Charles will excuse you, I'm sure.
We haven't had time to talk, and he'll have to be leaving for the office soon.''

''That's not necessary, it's only through the hedge,''
Rory murmured.

Kane, gripping her elbow hard enough to leave fin-
gerprints, steered her out the front door. Neither of
them spoke until they were standing under the dense
shade of the massive oak by her house.

''Rory, I want to apologize for—''

''Kane, you're hurting my arm.''

His grip instantly eased, but he didn't release her. A
truck rattled past. Two kids on bicycles rode by, yell-
ing back and forth. Rory felt perilously near tears for no
reason at all, and somehow, Kane seemed to sense this.

Gently he reached out and brushed a finger over the
vulnerable curve of her cheek. ''I'm sorry,'' he said
quietly. ''For a lot of things. I'm just beginning to realize how very many.''

With the feathery touch of his finger still burning her
skin, Rory couldn't think of a word to say. It took all
her strength not to walk into those warm, friendly arms
and stay there for the rest of her life.

''It's not your fault,'' she said, not sure what she was
referring to—only certain that none of her misery had
anything to do with Charles's best man.

He had kissed her. She was still reeling from it. That
wide, crooked mouth had touched hers, and now all she
could think of was the way he tasted, the way he felt

against her body, all hard and warm and exciting. She'd been half expecting Charles to take one look at her and accuse her of—

Oh, all sorts of wicked, wonderful things!

She looked away, embarrassed at what she was thinking, hoping Kane had forgotten about kissing her. Hoping even more that he hadn't. That he would do it again.

She could have wept when he lifted her chin and stared down into her eyes as if reading all her shameful secrets. Slowly his gaze moved over her features, making her acutely conscious of her every flaw. She opened her mouth to protest, but before she could utter a sound, he had joined his lips to hers.

Four
___

Like the first one, it started out as a gentle kiss. A sweet, summer-afternoon kind of kiss, comforting, reassuring. Then Kane groaned. His arms tightened, his mouth twisted and ground against Rory's lips, and before she quite knew what was happening to her, it had happened.

There was no room for embarrassment, for anger, certainly not for fear. Rory felt the stab of his tongue, tasted the tantalizing hint of coffee and something less tangible. Her knees turned to jelly. She had been kissed before, by at least half a dozen different men. Not a single one of them had ever affected her this way.

Kane's hands moved over her back, pressing her against his chest, his flat belly. In the background she was aware of the heat, the humidity, the lazy hum of insects and the dry sweetness of petunias as her senses came instantly, quiveringly alive. It was as if she'd been asleep for the past thirty years and was suddenly wakened by a clap of thunder. Her fingers curled in the warmth of his thick hair, and she realized that not only was she allowing this to happen to her—she was an eager participant.

By the time Kane dragged his mouth away, his breathing was decidedly ragged. There was a stunned look on his face. Rory stared dazedly into the depths of his warm, coffee brown eyes. Her gaze fell to his mouth, and it occurred to her that the habitual cynical twist of his lips was missing.

"Kane, I—" She didn't know what to say, she only knew that sound was safer than silence.

"Yeah. Me, too." He stepped back, a guarded look on his face, and then, without another word, he turned and cut through the hedge.

Rory watched until he disappeared before she turned and, like a sleepwalker, went inside. Ignoring the clutter of boxes she had tossed on the sofa before lunch, she stepped out of her shoes and made her way to her bedroom at the back of the house.

The air was stifling, but it never occurred to her to turn on the fan. Absently she lowered herself to the bentwood rocker she had brought with her from Kentucky. A bee droned around her lantana bush just outside the window, and she stared unseeingly at the sun-dappled screen.

Had she completely lost her mind?

Kane had kissed her. Twice. Not only had she let him do it, she had kissed him right back. Shaking off the effect, she made an effort to steer her thoughts into less dangerous channels, but they kept returning to...the kiss.

Why didn't Charles's kisses affect her the way Kane's did? Because Charles never kissed her the way Kane had just done.

Why not? Because she didn't appeal to him that way? Or because *he* didn't appeal to *her* that way?

Ridiculous! She was going to marry the man, wasn't she? Of course they appealed to each other! Charles was obviously experienced enough to know where a kiss like that could lead and was bending over backward not to alarm her.

Oh? And Kane was not so experienced? In a pig's eye!

How would Charles kiss her after they were married? What if she didn't like it? What if she couldn't bring herself to—?

Rory set the chair in motion, unaware that her breath had quickened. Had Kane's kiss been the kind that was referred to as a carnal kiss? She had read the term once in an article about virgins, who, according to the author, were more plentiful than was commonly supposed.

Of course, the same article had quoted Ovid as having said, "Chaste is she whom no one has asked."

But she'd been asked. She had experienced her share of wet kisses—sloppy, bruising attacks that had left her fearful and a bit disgusted. Certainly nothing she had ever experienced had borne any resemblance to Kane's kiss. Nor had she been left afterward with this—this aching, longing, *hungry* kind of feeling. Like a starving waif peering wistfully through a bakery window.

"Bosh!" she muttered. Acid stomach and a hyperactive imagination could produce all sorts of bizarre symptoms. Kane certainly hadn't felt anything. He had turned and walked away as if nothing had happened.

With brisk efficiency, Rory set about unpacking her boxes and parcels, putting away her wedding finery. By late afternoon she had almost managed to convince herself that she'd imagined the whole thing. Kane had given her a couple of quick pecks, and because she was tired, because she was under a certain amount of strain—because she was mad as blazes with that female steamroller next door—she had woven it into some airy-fairy storybook romance!

"Bosh," she muttered again.

Charles had a Rotary meeting, which let Aurora off the hook. Living next door to each other meant that they didn't actually date as often as they might have otherwise. They managed to see each other at least once a day. But Charles was unusually busy, and Rory was involved in several projects quite aside from getting ready for the fall term and getting ready for her wedding.

She had collected more than a dozen bags of assorted articles for the women's shelter. She had personally laundered the clothing, and it was ready to be delivered on her way to pick up the overstock from the secondhand bookstore, to be dropped off at the nursing home.

She sorted through the toiletries she had collected for the shelter, made a note of those that were in short supply and added several items from her own closet. Then she showered and went to bed. It was early, but if her lights were off, Charles wouldn't drop by when he returned from his meeting.

Dutifully, she cataloged Charles's sterling qualifications, counted her blessings and dozed off to sleep, hoping she wouldn't dream of Kane again tonight.

She did, of course, but then Kane disappeared and the dregs of an unpleasant memory began to take form. Instinctively she fought against it, but not before she smelled again the pungent smell of burning weed and heard the sound of laughter and dissonant music, heard again the sound of a slurred male voice whispering in her ear. Felt again the tentative touch of a hand on her thigh. . . .

Flopping over onto her stomach, Rory reached back and pulled the sheet over her head, despite the sultry heat of the late-July night. It had never really happened, she told herself. It was only a bad dream. A recurrent dream that had started shortly before her parents had taken her to live with her grandmother. At first she had resented being separated from her family, resented the rigid old woman and her rigid rules of behavior. But gradually, in the prim white house on Main Street, she had ceased to dream. After a while, she had all but forgotten the nightmares.

"Count your blessings," her grandmother used to tell her every night as she knelt beside the narrow white iron bed in the room up under the eaves. And dutifully she had given thanks for fried chicken and coconut pie; for brand new dresses bought from a department store, with socks and shoes to match; and for the library just four blocks east and one block over on Chestnut Street. She had tried to feel blessed because she lived in a real house instead of a drafty old converted barn with a dozen or more others who seemed to drift in and out of her life. But the truth was, sometimes she secretly missed the old days of running wild, of being everyone's child and no one's responsibility. There was something to be said for freedom, after all.

In the ensuing years she had learned that no one was ever truly free. Few were even secure. She was grateful to be engaged to marry a decent, kind man of whom her grandmother would've approved. Emma Truesdale had firmly believed that rules, respect and responsibility were the building blocks of civilization; courtesy the glue that held it all together.

Charles and Emma Truesdale were a lot alike.

"Grandma, wherever you are, be happy for me," she whispered into the still, hot night.

Irrelevantly she wondered what her grandmother would have thought of Kane Smith.

Rory was still in her pajamas, the *Journal* only half-read, when Charles rapped on her front screen door the next morning.

"It's open, come on in," she called out.

"You shouldn't leave your door unlocked, Aurora."

"I guess I forgot to hook it when I went out for the paper."

He kissed her on the forehead, straightened the calendar on the pantry door and said, "I'm sorry to bother you so early, my dear, but I wanted to speak to you before I left for the office."

Rory tried not to compare Charles's dry smack with the kiss she had shared with Kane. For one brief moment she considered throwing herself into Charles's arms and begging him to kiss her carnally.

Instead, she told him to help himself to coffee while she put on some clothes.

Not that she wasn't decently covered, but with Charles in his usual suit and tie, she felt rumpled, wrinkled and grumpy. The very last thing she felt was loverlike.

But then, obviously, neither did Charles. The moment she was back, wearing a yellow-and-white-gingham duster over her pajamas, he launched into his topic. "Aurora, Mother has decided to move back to town."

Rory's stomach convulsed around the honey-coated cereal, peanuts and chocolate milk she had just consumed. "That's...nice," she whispered.

Charles took a turn around her cluttered kitchen, one hand rucking back his coat to rest on his hip. "Yes, well—I suppose it's only natural for her to worry. I mean, the house is still in her name, you know."

"No, I—"

"Not that she doesn't think you'll take excellent care of it," he hastened to say. "It's just that Mother's getting older. It's only natural she should feel a need to have her family around her, and now that Eve's separated and moving back to the West Coast—"

Eve. Charles's sister. She would be here today. Oh, hell! "Then I guess your mother will be wanting to redecorate. I'd better get on with packing and sorting. When do you think she'll want to move in?"

"Aurora—my dear, I don't think you quite understand. I mean, it's not as if the house were cramped. It was built for a large family, but then Father died when Eve was five, and—well, these things happen, I suppose. We had hoped—that is, Suzanne and I were planning—" A flush stained his fair complexion, and he tugged at his gray striped tie. "Well, I suppose under the circumstances, that's hardly relevant. What I'm trying to say is—"

Rory's stomach growled. Probably the peanuts. Peanuts and chocolate were her two favorite foods, but in deference to her health, she made it chocolate milk and added a high-fiber cereal. The peanuts, she rationalized, supplied protein.

"Aurora, Mother plans to live with us."

This time her stomach really did revolt. "'Scuse me, Charles!" she cried and dashed into the bathroom.

Five minutes later, a pale and shaken Rory emerged. Charles had poured himself a cup of her coffee and was scanning the business section of the *Journal*. He jumped up, taking her arm and helping her into a chair as if she were suffering from a broken leg rather than a nervous stomach.

"Have you seen a doctor yet about that?"

"Last week. It's not anything catching, not even a full-fledged ulcer."

Yet, she added silently. She was tempted to tell him that the first thing the doctor had asked was if she could be pregnant, but Charles would be embarrassed. And so would she. They didn't even talk about things like that, much less *do* them.

"Well, I'm running late, but I thought you ought to know about—that is, perhaps you and Mother can get together later on today and talk about rooms and that sort of thing. Mother will have the front room and bath. It was hers before Suzanne and I were married, so it's only natural that she should want to spend her last years there."

Only natural? No way, José. Over several dead bodies! Why was it that whatever Charles decreed was always "only natural," and whenever she disagreed with him, she was being childish?

"We'll talk about it later," she parried. Feeling sick all over again, she forced a smile, realizing that she must be a better actress than she'd ever dreamed, because when she assured him that everything would work out, he expelled a gusty sigh of relief and left her with a peck on the cheek.

"Damn, hell and spit!" she mumbled, hooking the screen door after him and then deliberately unhooking it. "I refuse to—! How the devil can he expect me to—!"

Suddenly she slumped down into the kitchen chair and stared morosely at her own bare foot. She was still there twenty minutes later when Kane rapped on the door, pushed it open and came inside. She should have been embarrassed to see him again after the last time, but she was too utterly miserable to care.

"I guess he told you, then?" Kane sniffed the air. Detecting coffee, he got out a cup and filled it. "Top yours off?" he offered.

"I'm not even supposed to drink it," she replied dispiritedly.

"Family loyalty?"

"Incipient ulcer."

Without comment Kane studied her from across the cluttered table. Orderly by nature, she'd been sorting through some out-of-date reference books last week. "Ulcer, hmm? How long has this been going on?"

She shrugged. "A few weeks. A month, maybe."

So that's what the note about a doctor's appointment had been about. But a gynecologist? Why not an internist? "Special diet? Medication?"

"I don't take pills, and the latest expert opinion is that special diets don't do any good, anyway."

"The only thing certain about the latest expert opinion is that sooner or later it will be superseded by another expert opinion with another research grant."

She scowled at him, and he waved a placating hand. "Okay, okay! No pills, no bland foods. So how are you treating it ... by getting your life in order?"

Her head snapped up at that. "My life is in perfect order, thank you very much. Was there something in particular you wanted?"

Somewhat to his surprise Kane admitted to himself that what he wanted more than anything he could think of at that moment was to wipe those shadows from her eyes, to lift the corners of her soft, naked lips and to hear her laugh. And then he would go from there.

"So what's on the agenda for today? Packing away books? Picking out wedding music? Sending out last-minute invitations? Dusting the light fixtures?"

That elicited a fleeting smile, which gave him a feeling of relief all out of proportion to its brief duration. "Okay, then—why don't you go get dressed while I clean up in here." He reached for her cereal bowl, glanced at the remains of sodden cereal and what looked suspiciously like a peanut, all drowning in some opaque purplish liquid. He raised both eyebrows. "What's this, Hubbard's Herbal Remedy for Incipient Ulcers?"

"What it is is none of your business!" she snapped. "Kane, I've got a zillion things to do today, so why don't you go play best man somewhere else? Maybe Mrs. Banks can use a hand planning the rest of my life."

"I thought it was all planned," he said mildly. "Your beige silk, her backyard, a couple dozen Keep Off The Grass signs and Modene's organ, and then the three of you live happily ever after."

"Fine! Then go bake me a wedding cake! Or play hopscotch, I don't care, just leave me out of it! I wish to goodness," she lamented, "that Charles and I could just stop by a justice of the peace—alone!—and get this mess over and done with.''

Leaning his back against the refrigerator, Kane studied her as if he had never before seen a barefooted woman in rumpled pink pajamas and a yellow-checked duster, with a face full of beautiful freckles and her hair in a shaggy, streaky blond braid.

Rory intercepted his look and put her own interpretation on it. Men like Kane Smith, she told herself, were used to seeing women in silk and lace, with carefully tousled coiffures that took three hours to perfect! Men like Kane Smith...

''I'm sorry,'' she said with a sigh, ''I didn't mean to bite your head off, it's just—it's just that—''

''That you're not sleeping and your stomach's declared war, and you're feeling raw and uncertain because I kissed you and you kissed me back, and we both enjoyed it a little too much. Me, too, for what it's worth. I didn't sleep worth a damn last night.''

And then, before she could gather her wits to argue, he went on to say, ''I take it Charles just broke the news about your live-in mother-in-law. I can see where that wouldn't exactly make your day.''

Rory's shoulders slumped even more. ''I can't believe she really wants to live with us. She can't be much more than sixty, in spite of the way she acts. Doesn't she have a life of her own? What about her friends? What about—about her daughter? It's not as though she really needed us.'' She flung out her hands in a gesture of helplessness. ''It won't work, Kane. It's just not going to work, but how can I fix it without hurting her feelings and getting Charles all upset?''

Kane's mouth quirked in that familiar wry grin that made her heart flop over like a beached fish. ''Look, honey, we're not going to settle anything in the next half hour or so. Why don't you go shower and get dressed while I take care of these few dishes, and then we'll get down to brass tacks about what needs doing next."

"Kane, you don't need to wash my dishes. You don't need to do anything at all." *Unless you'd care to kidnap a certain blue-haired woman and deliver her to the other side of the world.*

"Ma'am, I beg to differ." Taking her firmly by the shoulders, Kane steered her into the hallway that led to the bathroom, which had been added on sometime just after the Second World War. "Because if we don't find something to keep my idle hands busy, they might just get us both in trouble."

"If you're at loose ends, why don't you offer your services to Mrs. Banks?" she suggested.

"Meaning no disrespect, but I'd rather eat worms." Her eyes lifted to his and a sparkle of laughter passed between them.

Twenty-five minutes later they met again in Rory's now-immaculate kitchen. The books were stacked neatly, sorted according to copyright date. "You really do need a newer dictionary, but I'd add on to the encyclopedias instead of trashing the set and starting over if I were you. Never know what the newer ones will leave out to make room for something else." Kane decided not to tackle her on the kind of food he'd found in her refrigerator and pantry. That could come later. But dammit, no wonder she was having trouble with her stomach!

"There's a limit to my shelf space, but you're right, of course. I'll probably keep them all." She looked around. "Wow! I can't remember the last time my kitchen looked so neat," Rory marveled.

"Air force training. First rule we learn is a place for everything and everything in its place. About those plants of yours..."

Rory felt considerably better in an ice blue sleeveless pique with her still-damp hair braided into a coronet. "My plants. Um...well, they're really not mine. I mean, they were started by my children this past spring, but I couldn't just let them die."

Right. Five yards of leafless sweet potato vine, a limp, shaggy carrot top, something that looked as if it were about to go foraging for food in her pantry, and a three-foot-tall stick with a single leaf on top. She was hopeless. So why the hell did that make him want to take her to bed?

It just didn't figure.

"Kane?" she began tentatively.

"Honey, just what the hell do you see in Charlie Banks?"

Her jaw fell. "You're supposed to be his friend!"

"Did he tell you Suzanne was my girl when he met her? Did he tell you we haven't seen each other since I served as best man at their wedding eleven years ago?"

"No—well, but..."

"Right. So cut all this friendship crap, because it's irrelevant."

"You mean you're not? Then why are you—"

"Why am I here? Why did I agree to stand up with poor Charlie again?"

"He's not poor Charlie, he's a—a very nice man!"

"Agreed. And I didn't say Charlie and I weren't friends. But I'm your friend, too, Rory. At least I want to be."

But Kane knew even as he spoke the words that he didn't want to be her friend. He wanted to be one hell of a lot more than that. And dammit, he was too late! He'd never been any angel—there were few rules he hadn't broken, but somehow, stealing poor old Charlie's woman right out from under his nose was too much, even if Charlie had done the same thing to him back in their salad days.

Unless, Kane rationalized, it was the only way to save two people from making a world-class mistake. In that case a guy might almost look on it as a mission. A mandate. An obligation.

Nah, this was crazy! It didn't happen this fast. "Look, if I'm going to help you through the latest crisis, why don't we sit down and make up a list of ground rules, then go next door and present 'em to Mama Banks and then get the hell out of town before she blows? If you're going to have to share Charlie with her, you're going to have to stand up to her right off the bat, else she'll use you for a doormat."

Rory shoved her fingers through her braided top-knot and scratched. "Do you think if I went back to bed and woke up again an hour from now, none of this will have happened?"

"Chicken," he taunted softly.

"You betcha!"

"All right, what else is left to do if you're not game to go lock horns with Maddie Banks?"

"You have to ask?" Dear Lord, she was even beginning to react to the sound of his voice! It was seventy-four degrees already, and she had goose bumps all over!

"Right. So get your lists and we'll sort through them, knock off the quickest first, so you won't have so many hanging over your head."

"Is that your system?"

"Guaranteed stress buster." His eyes were warm, his face, with its angular, irregular features, as nonthreatening as an Easter bunny, Rory told herself.

So why did she feel threatened? Why did she have this uneasy feeling that her entire life had changed the minute Kane Smith had walked through her hedge and she had backed into him with her bare foot and doused him with scrub water?

By a quarter of twelve they had decided on the traditional wedding march and a medley of Cole Porter tunes which would be played as quiet background music while the small wedding party attended whatever reception Eve and Mrs. Banks insisted on having.

They had decided on a single attendant for her, and she had decided—depending on whether or not any of her family actually showed up—to ask her baby sister, Misty, to be it. Three would be just too much for a small, private ceremony, and besides, Fauna...

Well, one couldn't always depend on Fauna to behave.

"And in case they don't make it, I can ask Charles's sister. What's she like?" Rory had slipped off her white sandals and twisted her ankles around the front legs of the kitchen chair. She nibbled on her pencil while Kane poured them glasses of iced... whatever.

"Sharp. Attractive. Ambitious."

Rory snuffed out a surge of completely unwarranted jealousy. "You know her pretty well then?"

Kane grinned. "I doubt she'll even remember me."

"Oh. Well, the friend from school I'd normally ask is teaching English in Prague, so I hope Eve won't mind stepping in at the last minute if my family doesn't show. They might not, you know. They're—unpredictable."

"Eve won't mind. She's a good sort."

Rory dusted her hands together. "That's one more thing settled, then. It's not as if it were any big deal. I mean, a few minutes, and it'll all be over."

Kane set her glass down in front of her. "Not quite," he said with an odd sort of smile.

Rory lifted a questioning brow. "Oh. You mean the reception. Okay, so we'll drink champagne and make a few toasts, and *then* it'll be over."

"Rory—" Kane straddled the chair across the table and leaned his forearms on the cloth-covered surface. "A few words, a few toasts, and it'll all be just beginning. Your life with Charlie."

She swallowed visibly. "I know that," she mumbled, twisting a thread in the fringe of the daisy-print tablecloth.

"I'm not so sure you do. Honey, listen to me. If you have any doubts about it, now's the time to sing out."

"What doubts could I possibly have? Charles is a wonderful man. He's the kind of a man every woman dreams of marrying. He's—he's steady, mature, reliable—he's kind and undemanding and—"

"Undemanding? Now there's an interesting specification for a bridegroom. Do you mean he won't demand that you give up teaching, or he won't demand that you drop everything twice a day and hop into the sack with him to slake your mutual passions?"

Rory felt the heat rise up her chest until even her scalp prickled with embarrassment. "How—dare—you?" she whispered.

Kane laughed. And then his laughter faded as he realized she actually meant it. "How *dare* I? Rory, women haven't used that phrase for at least fifty years. Men dare most anything these days. Women dare even more.

No taboos. It's the new freedom from repression, hadn't you noticed? You've been liberated, lady."

"Excuse me," she muttered. Shoving her chair back, she rushed from the room, leaving Kane staring after her. When the bathroom door slammed, he stood, torn between going after her and getting the hell out of there.

But when he heard the pitiful sounds of retching, he didn't hesitate. "Rory—honey, we've got to do something about this skittish belly of yours."

She was on her knees, sitting back on her heels when he found her, looking green and shaken. Beads of perspiration glistened on her face, and Kane's heart went out to her. He lifted her up, not surprised when she didn't protest. From the looks of her, she couldn't have swatted a gnat.

"Okay now, honey, let's get you laid out somewhere, and you can nap for a while."

"I hate this," Rory whispered miserably. "I hate having you see me this way, I hate being sick in my stomach, I hate July, but most of all, I hate weddings."

"Shh, sure you do, love, sure you do. At a time like this, a woman needs a mother, but I reckon since she's not here, I'll just have to pinch hit." She had left her shoes under the kitchen table. Kane laid her on her bed, removed her wristwatch, unpinned her braid and unfastened the high neck of her sleeveless cotton dress. Deftly he worked the dress under her body and over her head, and draped it over the back of the old-fashioned rocking chair.

Her slip was white. Cotton. He didn't know they even made things like that in this century. She was shivering, and it was all he could do not to climb into bed and warm her the quickest way he knew how. But that, as they said in medical circles, would be contraindicated.

Most *definitely* contraindicated!

"Want me to peel off your slip and cover you up?"

Her eyes widened alarmingly. "Leave me alone! Don't you dare—"

"Hey, hey, just offering." Lifting both hands, palms out, Kane stepped away from the bed.

"I'm sorry. I don't feel well."

She looked lousy. Beautiful and vulnerable and unhappy, and Kane knew he was in way over his head. "Who's your doctor?"

"I don't need a doctor. All I need is to be left alone."

Right. And all he needed was to have stayed in Key West and played games with that redhead, what's-her-name, for a couple more weeks. Just two weeks, and he would've been safe.

Instead, he'd blundered into a situation he might never be free of. The worst of it was that he didn't even want to be free.

He wet a washcloth and gently wiped off her face, her throat and her hands. He smoothed her hair back from her forehead, trying to ignore the silken feel of it, the transparent look to her skin. Her eyes were closed, but he knew damned well she wasn't asleep.

Lady, lady, what have you done to me? he thought silently. For a long time, he stood there watching her. After a while, her breathing evened out. Once her eyelids flickered up, and for just a moment he thought he glimpsed something like panic in her eyes, but then she smiled. A moment later she slept again.

Five

Kane was still sitting in the chintz-covered easy chair when Madeline Banks called through the screen door. "Miss Hubbard? Aurora?"

"She's lying down, Mrs. Banks," said Kane. Reluctantly he rose and crossed to open the door.

The expression on the woman's face was enough to tell him that he should have gone back through the hedge long before now. Gone somewhere, at least. For Rory's sake. Because she would be the one to bear the brunt of this woman's suspicions. And knowing Maddie Banks, it would be a pretty hefty brunt.

"Aurora's not feeling well. I didn't like to leave her alone."

"I . . . see."

Madeline Harrison Banks was a large woman. Handsome at best, impressive at the very least. In all the years he had lived next door, Kane had never seen her less than flawlessly groomed, her pale hair neatly coiffed, her modest pearl jewelry in perfect taste. She wore suits and cashmere sweaters in the wintertime, cotton pastels in the summer, sometimes with a matching cotton cardigan. She didn't perspire. She didn't wrinkle. Not even the most suspicious salesclerk would have hesitated for a single minute to accept her personal check.

Right now Kane wished her in Hades.

"Has Miss—Aurora seen her physician?"

"I believe so."

"May I inquire as to the nature of her illness?"

"Upset stomach." If Rory wanted the old bird to know the particulars, she could enlighten her. Personally, Kane would just as soon tell her to go jump rope.

Three rooms down the hall, Rory lay with her eyes closed, aware of the murmur of voices, too drained to know or care who was in her house. It wouldn't be Charles, that much she did know. Charles was too busy. He had been too busy almost since the very moment she had agreed to marry him.

It hadn't always been that way—not that he had exactly swept her off her feet. But at least he'd courted her. He had most definitely courted her. Even with her lack of experience, Rory had known she was being courted, and for once in her life she had relaxed and enjoyed it. Charles was that kind of man. He invited trust, and she had trusted him.

But once she had agreed to marry him, the courtship had ended. She'd been puzzled and a little bit hurt, but he'd explained that if they were going to make time for a wedding trip, he would need to use his time wisely right up until they were married.

Evidently, using his time wisely did not include playing a game he had already won. It was called being taken for granted. She'd heard of it. What woman hadn't? Oddly enough, it hadn't bothered her nearly as much as it should have, and maybe she should have been bothered. Courtship was a time of testing, wasn't it?

How could they know they would suit each other if they didn't push the parameters just a bit? Everyone did. Most couples didn't wait to get engaged before they went to bed together. And she'd braced herself to do it, only he hadn't asked.

And now, the longer she waited, the more impossible it seemed.

Rory wasn't totally without experience. She had dated occasionally in college. Group dates, usually. Movie dates and parties. But the groups usually split up into couples, and any pair who wasn't sleeping together was made to feel de trop. Same with the parties. She hardly drank at all, didn't sleep around, didn't do drugs, which had made her a drag as far as most boys were concerned.

She did enjoy movies, only invariably she would find something funny in the most serious drama and laugh at the wrong time.

Really, being young hadn't been all it was cracked up to be. She had never known what boys expected from her, never known what to expect of them. Life was no Annette Funicello beach movie, she did know that. Not life in the nineties, at least.

Rory had almost given up on romance when she had moved to North Carolina and got a job teaching at the same school where her old college roommate taught.

Practically the first person she'd met was Charles Banks.

He'd been married then, of course. It had never occurred to her to think of him as anything other than a neighbor and landlord. Suzanne had occasionally dropped over to chat, but other than that, she'd had little contact with the young Bankses.

And then Suzanne had suddenly died. The whole community had been stunned, for she'd been perfectly well the week before.

Six months later Charles had asked her to go to a business banquet as his partner, and she had. After that they had dated occasionally, either a movie and dinner or the monthly dinner dance at Charles's club. He was lonely, he claimed, and Rory had been lonely, too.

It was on a Friday in late April, following the annual clean-hands-and-company-manners tea party Rory gave for her second-graders, that Charles proposed. She had taken the leftover cream cheese sandwiches and iced vanilla wafers home, along with the real china cups and saucers and linen napkins she had rented for the occasion. She and Charles had sat on the front porch, swinging and nibbling, talking about nothing in particular, when he suddenly turned to her and asked her to marry him.

She had nearly inhaled a frosted vanilla wafer. By the time he had slapped her on the back and handed her his handkerchief to mop her steaming eyes, the moment had lost any semblance of romance.

"Well, will you?" he asked.

"Charles, are you sure you want me?"

"My dear, I think we'd suit admirably. Of course, if you're looking for a swashbuckling hero to sweep you off your feet, I'm afraid that lets me out." He had turned to her then with a self-deprecating smile she found utterly disarming. "But if you're willing to settle for a man who admires you a great deal, a man who respects you and who can afford to take good care of you, why then, you don't need to look any further. Give it some thought, will you?"

He had kissed her then, and she'd waited for the fireworks. In their absence, she had smiled and hidden her disappointment, telling herself that things would heat up once she got used to the idea of being in love.

They never had. Charles evidently wasn't a passionate man. Or maybe he was just showing her respect. She'd seen him get pretty turned on by actuarial tables. Downright passionate about an arson insurance swindle. Maybe after they were married he would warm up.

And maybe not. Maybe he'd been drawn to her because neither of them had a particularly strong sex drive. Like to like. Rory firmly believed there was more than a kernel of truth behind those old sayings.

Oh, yeah? What about opposites attracting?

Her mind flew instantly to Kane Smith, and with a grunt of disgust, she sat up in bed and waited to see if her stomach was going to rebel. When it didn't, she cautiously slid her feet onto the crocheted rug beside the bed. With a million and one things to do, she didn't have time to coddle herself. Those bags to deliver, for one, and the books to collect. And this was the last Saturday of the month. Tonight was the club dance. They always went, because so many of Charles's clients and business associates would be there. He'd told her once that his membership was a business write-off. Somehow, after that, their club dates had never seemed quite so romantic.

"Rats," she muttered, twisting her ragged braid on top of her head and anchoring it with half a dozen hairpins.

Five minutes later, Rory presented herself in her own living room. Madeline Banks sat gingerly on the golden oak straight chair, peering at her as if she expected her to be broken out in spots.

Kane levered himself out of the easy chair, his eyes warm and encouraging. "Sure you feel like getting up?"

Rory fought against a perfectly irrational urge to hurl herself into his arms. He had waited. She suddenly felt like weeping over that small kindness.

Madeline Banks said, "Miss Hubbard, my own physician is still practicing. I'm sure if I were to call him, he'd be glad to work you in."

"Thank you, Mrs. Banks, but I'm just fine. It was only a nervous stomach. I know better than to drink coffee, but—"

"Charles asked me to go over several matters with you this morning, but I'm sure it will wait until after lunch."

It could wait until after the martians landed, but that wouldn't solve anything. "No, I'd just as soon get it over with. I hate loose ends. They pile up, and then, first thing you know—" She shut her mouth firmly. The woman made her nervous, and when she was nervous, she invariably babbled, which made her feel even worse.

Kane walked the two women back to the house next door. There he bid Mrs. Banks a good morning, winked at Rory and left.

Feeling like a passenger on the Titanic, watching the last lifeboat pull away, Rory turned resolutely to the older woman. "Mrs. Banks, Charles tells me you're planning to move back to Tobaccoville."

* * *

Three hours later—Mrs. Banks having clearly staked out her territory over Rory's polite protests—they were still in the front parlor when Eve arrived. For one guilt-ridden instant she wondered why she hadn't had the foresight to get engaged to an orphan.

His mother was a streamroller. No matter what Rory said, Madeline Banks went on as if she hadn't even opened her mouth! And this, she reminded herself, was only the beginning!

Evelyn Banks Patelli Sanders was a tall, long-legged, female version of her brother. Rory was prepared to like her, for Charles's sake. Perhaps she could talk some sense into her mother, because so far Rory hadn't been able to make a dent.

"So you're Charles's little schoolteacher."

Rory didn't consider herself anyone's little anything, but managed not to say so. "I've been looking forward to meeting you, Mrs. Sanders." Which was a bald-faced lie. She was fed up to the back teeth with Charles's family... but then, he hadn't met hers yet.

Eve laughed. "You're prettier than Mother said. Lord, I'm bushed! I need a drink and a long, cool soak, and then maybe I'll feel human again. Mother, come up with me while I unpack. You won't believe Tom's latest settlement offer!"

"I'm sure Miss Hubbard will excuse us, won't you, dear? I'll have Carrie take your things up. The east room I believe, since you've always been such an early riser."

Eve loped up the stairs, giving lie to her claim of fatigue, and Mrs. Banks disappeared to find Carrie Mountjoy, leaving Rory standing in the hallway feeling about as useful as half a slice of cold toast leftover from breakfast.

She managed to get her deliveries made and lingered a few minutes to talk to two of the residents of the nursing home, but all afternoon, Rory's stomach threatened rebellion. Back home she made herself sip a mug of her father's alfalfa, fenugreek, chamomile and peppermint tea. She stared at the overgrown, anemic vegetables in her kitchen window, shook her head in defeat and went and cleaned out her underwear drawer, throwing out all the panties with tired elastics. At least she'd accomplished something.

At four-thirty, Charles called. "Mother said you weren't feeling well this morning, dear."

"Just my nervous stomach. So far I haven't broken out in spots."

"Dear God, Aurora, you're not—"

"No, I'm not, Charles! I was just joking. Really."

"You're sure? Kane and Eve can go on without us tonight, and I'll come over and sit with you if you'd rather. Or Mother will."

Over my dead body, Rory thought with a bleak smile. "No, it's okay, Charles. I feel just fine now. In fact, I've been sorting out things and getting organized to move. Uh—your mother and I had a long talk this morning, did she tell you?"

"She said you made a lot of headway."

Rory's laugh had a slightly desperate sound. "Oh, indeed we did!" The headway being, she added silently, that now we know which Mrs. Banks intends to run things and which one is supposed to shut up and be a good little girl.

Rory was utterly disgusted with herself. After the first two hours, she'd actually heard herself agreeing that yes, the tea roses were superb, and yes, she really did appreciate understatement when it came to landscaping, and yes this and yes that until she was thoroughly disgusted with her own cowardice.

The truth was she liked frowsy, overgrown gardens and fragrant, old-fashioned roses on long, floppy canes that sprawled halfway across a yard. She had so looked forward to breaking up those boring rectangular beds and putting in iris and ramblers and even a vegetable garden.

She had looked forward, in fact, to redecorating the entire Banks estate, inside and out, into something more cheerful and less formal. Including Charles himself.

Fat chance!

"Seven-thirty, then?" Charles asked.

"Yes, all right. Fine," she said tiredly. "I'll be ready."

By 7:25, Rory was dressed in her high-necked, loose-waisted, rose-and-white-print lawn, her hair twisted up the back of her head in a tidy roll. She splashed on her favorite light scent, and put on her jewelry—the garnet earrings her grandmother had given her and Charles's modest Tiffany-set diamond engagement ring.

But ready? She was so far from ready it wasn't even funny.

Rory had truly intended to see her gynecologist this week, but she had lost her nerve. If only she and Charles could talk on a really personal level, she could just tell him the truth and they could deal with it sensibly.

"Charles, dearest," she could hear herself saying, "it just so happens that I'm still a virgin, and the older I get, the more nervous I get about . . . you know. *It*. So would you mind too much if I went to Dr. Mallett for a very minor operation so that we won't have to worry about pain and blood and all that yucky stuff?''

Twisting the ring on her finger, she sighed, wondering for the hundredth time why the devil she hadn't just done what most women did sooner or later—usually much sooner than the age of thirty!—and had herself a quiet little affair?

It wasn't for lack of opportunity. That football player she had dated her first week at State had scared the bejabbers out of her. Now she almost wished she had given in to his demands. At least she wouldn't be suffering from all this silly anxiety.

Not to mention the bizarre dreams she'd been having just lately—and not about Charles, either!

By the time the two couples arrived, the monthly dinner dance was in full spate, the noise level attesting to the fact that the bar had been open since noon. Madeline Banks had declined, claiming letters to write. Eve and Rory left the men waiting while they visited the ladies' room, where Eve touched up her flawless makeup and then offered her compact to Rory. ''It's fairly heavy duty. Might even cover those freckles of yours.''

''Thanks, but I've given up on them by now.'' Their eyes met in the mirror and Rory braced herself for the questions she saw there.

''How long have you and Charles known each other?''

''Oh—for several years now. We met when I moved here from a little town near Lexington, Kentucky. To teach. School.''

''What about Kane?''

''What about him?''

"You two seem to hit it off pretty well."

Quite an assumption, Rory thought, seeing that it was based solely on the thirty-five-minute drive to the club tonight.

"We haven't known each other but a few days. He seems . . . nice."

Eve atomized a whiff of Poison between her breasts and dropped the purse spray into her gray silk bag. "Nice?" she repeated. "Darling, flowers are nice. Candy is nice. Kane Smith is utterly delicious! I can't imagine how I could have forgotten him all these years, but then, I was something of a snob back then. The Smiths next door were rather beneath my notice." Eve grinned, and for reasons Rory couldn't begin to fathom, she found the woman slightly more likable.

"I expect we'd better get back," she said, not wanting to talk about Kane Smith with anyone, particularly not a woman who considered him . . . delicious?

Oh, yes, decidedly delicious. *Disastrously* delicious!

They ate, and five minutes after their table was cleared and another bottle of wine was served, Rory couldn't have named a single thing she had eaten. Her mind skittered like a water bug over the lists of things still to be done before she was ready to surrender her name, her identity, her home and her body.

Mercy, why had she worn such a high-necked dress! Even a couple of layers of thin cotton were too much on a sultry night like this!

Thunder rumbled suddenly, and she flinched.

"Are you all right, my dear?" Charles asked.

"Fine. Wonderful!" She beamed at him, shutting out the sight of Eve leaning toward Kane with her hand on the sleeve of his tan linen jacket.

"You're not!" Eve exclaimed. "Kane, you really are, aren't you? Why didn't someone tell me?"

With a sigh of irritation, Charles turned to his sister. "Not what, are what, and tell you what?"

"Brother, did you know that our Kane is *the* Kane Smith?"

Rory's gaze went from Eve to Kane to Charles and back to Kane. He looked irritated.

"If you're finished, Eve, why don't we dance?" he growled.

Rory watched them edge through the round tables toward the area where some dozen or so other couples were dancing. "Have I missed something?" she asked.

"Nothing important, my dear. Do you feel up to dancing?"

Now it was Rory's turn to be irritated. "I keep telling you, Charles, I'm just fine!"

After two numbers, they switched partners. Rory wasn't sure who had instigated the switch, but she was fairly certain it wasn't Eve.

Kane led her onto the floor, holding her loosely. Neither of them spoke as she effortlessly matched her steps to his. Within seconds, the slight pressure of his hand on her back had heated up until she almost moved closer just to escape it.

"Is it going to rain, do you think?" she asked, more than a hint of desperation in her voice.

"Probably."

Someone bumped against her, throwing her against his chest, and she backed off as if she'd been scorched. Kane's mouth twisted in a familiar mocking smile, and she felt her face begin to burn as well. "I think the band must be stuck," she murmured.

"Give up?"

"If you don't want to dance anymore—"

"I don't," he said gruffly. "Not with you."

Rory was unprepared for the sharp stab of pain. When she found her voice, she said, "Well, that's certainly plain speaking."

They were standing near one of the French windows. Kane's hand was still resting on her waist, her fingers tucked into the palm of his other hand. But instead of moving away, he moved closer just as a sudden flash of lightning turned the greens outside to a ghastly fluorescent shade.

As thunder crashed around them, Rory's stricken gaze flew to his. "Kane, I—"

"Don't say it."

"Say what?" she whispered, no longer in control of her own mind.

"Whatever you were going to say, don't. Lady, I'm hanging on to my company manners by a split hair right now, and if you move—if you so much as speak—I might just—"

Rory's eyes closed. Her breathing apparatus went on strike. Every pore of her skin drank in the essence of the man who was gripping her waist with one hand and crushing her fingers with the other.

He was going to kiss her, she thought dazedly, right here in public. The rest of the world quietly disappeared as she shut her eyes and swayed toward him.

And then the sound system crackled, and the band leader made an announcement. "Okay, folks, I've been asked to remind any of you who left your tops down or your sunroofs open that it's raining puppies and kittens over in Stokes County, headed this way. Now, for the rest of you lucky people, here's an old Lawrence Welk polka to drown out the thunder. And-a one-a, and-a two-a.''

Rory's eyes snapped open. She felt as if she'd run hard all the way up to the top of Pilot Mountain. Kane's hand dropped, and she turned away and hurried back to the table.

Charles stood up at her approach. "It's getting late," he said. "I'd just as soon not have to drive home in the rain."

"I'm ready." She collected her small bag, trying to ignore the man who brushed past her. Because Charles had driven, Kane and Eve had no choice but to leave with them.

Although Eve made her feelings obvious. "Gawd, you haven't changed a bit, have you, brother? A few drops of rain and you think the sky's falling."

"Aurora's not feeling well," Charles said, making Rory feel even worse.

The rest of the drive was made in silence. Halfway home, the bottom fell out, and no one could have been heard over the pounding rain, anyway. Enclosed in the confines of Charles's sedan, Rory could almost feel the unspoken emotions swirling around her. Strife had always made her ill. She'd do almost anything to avoid it.

But there was worse to come. "Oh, no," she whispered as they turned the corner and she caught sight of a familiar van gleaming wetly under the streetlight. It couldn't be. It was way too soon. The wedding was over a week off. Besides, they would have called first. Maybe it was another van that had pulled over to wait for the rain to slack off.

But even in this deluge, there was no mistaking the rainbow emblazoned across the side of the big yellow van parked in front of Charles's house, nor the neon green logo underneath.

Her family had arrived. Now, when she was having powerful second thoughts about the whole thing, her family had arrived for the wedding!

Six

An hour later Rory led her parents through the hedge to the bungalow. Following her carefully drawn map, they had arrived just after Rory and the others had left for the club. When no one had responded to Bill's banging on both doors and calling her name, Peace had quietly gone next door to inquire.

And the rest, Rory told herself, fighting the hysterical urge to giggle, was history. Madeline Banks might be a match for a Fort Bragg drill sergeant, but she was no match for the Hubbards, en masse. Despite the fact that they had more or less embraced the establishment they had once so despised, Bill and Sunny Hubbard were light years apart from the Madeline Bankses of this world.

There was the way they looked at things, to start with, Rory reminded herself. To Sunny, a staunch believer in karma, everyone, from the Queen of England to the lowliest earthworm, was simply playing out his chosen role on this particular plane of existence, and wasn't it a kick? Life, that was. A real kick!

Bill's more esoteric beliefs were kept pretty much undercover these days. While he wasn't a member of any chamber of commerce so far as Rory knew, neither was he above joining if he thought it would further the righteous cause of herbalism.

Actually, Bill had never entirely forgotten that it was his parents' hard-earned money that had afforded him the opportunity to drop out of mainstream life back in the mid-sixties. His vows of poverty had not, of course, extended to his six-hundred-dollar guitar, his Karmin Ghia, or his imported, water-buffalo sandals. Rory suspected that in the secret depths of his flower-child soul, there had always lurked a nasty seed of capitalism. He had made the transition with surprising grace, never quite surrendering his free spirit. For a graying, balding, middle-aged man, he looked quite attractive in his white ducks, his tie-dyed shirt and a single string of African trade beads.

She wondered what he thought of Charles. And then she wondered what he thought of Kane, and wondered why she even wondered.

Sunny had changed little over the years. Rory could never quite picture her growing up in that prim house on Main Street, wearing starchy little dresses, patent leather Mary Janes and ruffled socks. Sunny was an original. She designed and made her own clothes, her own foods, her own music—her own life. Sometimes Rory felt as though Sunny were the child, she the mother. Right now she could have used someone a little more conventional in the role. Sunny's advice on sex, for instance, just might be a little more unorthodox than Rory was ready for.

The Hubbards dumped their bags—a Hartman, a Louis Vuitton and an assortment of ratty-looking backpacks—in the guest room, while Rory adjusted the shades and turned down the bedspread. "There's an electric fan on the closet shelf. You'll probably want to use it."

"Honey, are you sure you know what you're doing? Haven't you noticed his aura? It's—"

"Bill, do you want some tea before you turn in?" Rory offered, pretending not to hear her mother's warning. "I have some of that Nirvanaland Special you sent me. It tastes like rosemary-flavored beer, but it might help you sleep in a strange bed."

"It's the hops."

"The what?"

"Well, the catnip, too, I reckon. You think it needs more rosemary? The passion flower was Sunny's idea, but—"

"Daddy, the tea's just fine! The bathroom's across the hall, and there are towels in the—"

"It's sort of grayish," mused Sunny. "Not unhealthy, exactly, but sort of . . . thin, I guess you could say."

"The *tea?*" Rory and Bill demanded together.

Sunny blinked her dense, colorless lashes. At forty-eight, freckled like Rory, with the same streaky tan hair, she could have passed for Rory's age. "What tea? I was talking about Charles's aura. Lovey, you do know he's completely wrong for you, don't you? What's his birth date? I'll cast a quick solar chart. Have I progressed yours lately? I'd better do that, too, but I can already tell you where your problems are. He's got an awful lot of Capricorn, hasn't he? Not that Capricorns can't be wonderful—Venus people always are—but, lovey, he won't make you happy. Not even if he has a moon in Cancer, but then, he doesn't have the face for that. I wouldn't be at all surprised to see his Saturn sitting plunk down on one leg of your cardinal square, either. Now, if it were that beautiful Scorpio you were mar—''

''Mo—ther!'' Rory exclaimed. ''Charles and I are perfectly suited! He's everything I ever wanted in a husband, and I'm the luckiest woman alive that he'll even have me!''

Sunny's mobile face crumpled, and she held out her arms to her daughter. ''Oh, lovey, you're hurting, aren't you? All mixed up and nowhere to turn for help. Well, never you mind, Sunny's here now, and everything is going to work out just fine. We'll just follow our instincts, and it'll all settle into the proper pattern. Trust me, love—you know I'm never wrong about these things, am I, Bill?''

Rory gave up. When Sunny was in her Earth Mother mode, it was best just to pretend to go along with her.

Eventually they were settled, and Rory escaped to her own bed, where she rehashed the events of the evening. It wasn't a *total* disaster. Not yet, at least, she thought, nursing a mug of her father's Nirvanaland Special between her hands. Fauna had been only slightly outrageous, teasing both Charles and Kane, but that was her way. She was lazy, she was the world's greatest slob, she was a tease and a flirt, but she was so pretty and so good-natured, everyone forgave her, even on the rare occasions when her mischief went a bit too far.

Of course, Mrs. B had rucked up like a starched petticoat but had been too polite to say anything. Sunny and Bill had been blithely unaware, of course, and Misty had distracted attention with her standard lecture on the evils of red meat.

Tomorrow or the next day they'd be subjected to another on the evils of white meat, and then any meat at all. It was a toss-up which would follow—fur coats, ozone holes or animal experiments. Misty was passionate about all her causes. Since it was July and hot as Hades, they'd probably be spared the fur lecture.

Poor Charles—he hadn't known whether to take her seriously or not. Rory could have stepped in, but he would have to learn to accept the Hubbards as they were. Rory loved them all dearly. She would have given her life for them, but she wasn't sure she could explain them to someone like Madeline Banks. How did one explain a mother who saw the universe as a stage, and all its creatures as players, or a father who, like Icarus, had flown a little too high a few times too often? How to explain a sister who was a militant vegetarian, or one who called herself a musical ecdysiast and made a living at it, simply because it didn't require a degree and it allowed her to sleep late mornings?

At least Eve and Peace had hit it off. The last Rory had seen of those two they'd been comparing notes on settlements and lawyers. Goodness only knew what had happened after she and her parents had left last night. She had a fleeting vision of waking up to find herself disengaged, evicted, hustled along with her family into the Heavenly Herbals van and escorted to the county line under uniformed guard.

The last thought on her mind before she slipped into an emotionally exhausted sleep was, *What beautiful Scorpio?*

* * *

Rory awoke the next morning to find her nice neat kitchen in ruins and both her parents missing. She was still in the process of reconstructing what could have happened when Misty wandered into the house.

"So this is your nest, hmm? Cozy. If it were mine, I'd compost those poor sick plants and knock out that wall over there and put in a big bay window, and then I'd paint everything, including the furniture, white. What do you think?"

"I think Sunny and Bill must've rigged a bomb to go off under my kitchen counter and then skipped town."

"Oh, Bill's working on something big. He's got this great idea for a breakfast food with raw oatmeal and wheat germ and raisins and sunflower seeds, if he can just figure out how to package it so that the wheat germ and seeds don't go rancid, and—"

"Please—it's too early for breakfast food formulas." Rory sank into a chair and raked her hair back from her face. She hadn't slept well, which was nothing new. As a consequence, she felt like heck warmed over. Which was also nothing new. "If they went next door, I don't want to hear about that, either."

"I think they went to some mill or other to see what kind of grinding equipment they had—steel or stone. They stopped by to see if we needed the van this morning, but Eve and Peace are going shopping, and Fauna's still in bed."

"Did Mrs. Banks...say anything after we left last night?"

"About what?"

"About—you know. About *us*. About me. About my family!"

Misty shrugged. At twenty-two, she was small and blonder than Rory, with wide blue eyes and a dimpled chin. One of her big sorrows in life was that no one took her seriously. "She'd hardly say it to me, would she? I mean, what's to say? We're decent, law-abiding, self-supporting citizens." Misty had recently taken over the bookkeeping for Hubbard's Heavenly. "What's not to like?"

"Oh, nothing, nothing at all," said Rory tiredly. "If you overlook the fact that our parents smoked every vegetable they could lay hands on and worshipped trees and turned childbirth into a spectator sport and—"

"Under trees, not necessarily the trees themselves. And as for childbirth, lots of people do that. They call it bonding."

"I was only *three* when Peace was born. I didn't *want* to be bonded to a wet, red, screaming piglet!"

"Wow," Misty exclaimed softly. "Grandma really screwed you up, didn't she? I always thought you were kind of different, but I put it down to being raised by a woman who wore a lace-up corset. Maybe it's your age, you reckon? Or maybe you're just trying too hard to fit into Charles's world?"

"I'm just trying to fit into *any* world," Rory snapped. She had given up trying to fit her own two worlds together—the world of neat brick houses with neat picket fences, where people went to Sunday School on Sunday, and a matinee on Saturday afternoon, where grass was for mowing and not for smoking, where people wore bathing suits when they swam and everyone knew exactly who their own parents were. "Sorry, Misty, I didn't mean to bite your head off. Oops—sorry about that, too. Meat, I mean." Rory, while she didn't share her sister's dietary beliefs, didn't make an issue of her own, either. "It's just so—I mean, I've just been—"

"I understand. It's not enough you're marrying a mama's boy, now his mama's moving in on you. You could probably deal with it better if you hadn't been clogging your system with the flesh of all those dead animals all these years, but—"

"Don't start on me. Misty Morning Hubbard, just don't you start on me, or I swear I'll—I'll—"

"Keep me in after school? Make me wash the blackboards? Sorry, hon, but I'm just telling it like it is. You're so stressed out you look like hell dug deeper."

"Thanks, I really needed that."

"Just kidding. For an overinhibited, overconscientious, thirty-one-year-old—"

"For your information, I turned thirty less than a month ago!"

"—thirty-year-old meat eater, you're in tolerable shape, but, honey, you've got to be crazy if you think you can make it with Charles. That walking calculator's got to be the second worst thing that ever happened to you."

"Oh? And just what do you consider the first worst?" Rory asked coolly.

"Grandma Truesdale. She never really forgave Sunny for running away, and personally I think she took it out on you. Or maybe it was that jerk who tried to rape you when you were—"

"Misty!"

"Well, he did. I know everyone pretends you were sent to Kentucky just because Sunny thought her mother needed someone to live with her, but Peace was there, and she was old enough to know what was going on. Good thing she had a great set of lungs, or you'd probably be even more messed up than you are. She screamed for Bill, and the next thing we all knew, you were on your way north to Grandma's, and that mushroom brain and his funky little pipes was flat out of there."

"I don't remember any of it," Rory said flatly. "Have you had breakfast yet?"

"All I'm saying, Rory, is don't make the mistake of marrying some undersexed clotheshorse just because you got a bad scare once when you were a kid. It happens, you know. Maybe more than you think. Just don't let it ruin the rest of your life."

"Are you finished?"

Misty sighed and reached for the peanuts. "I just want you to be happy, and I'm not sure Charles is—"

"Charles is a fine man. I intend to be extremely happy."

"Sure you do. You're all aglow just thinking about it, aren't you? Rory, he's *dull*. So he's good-looking— so what? He's got a spreadsheet mentality."

"I happen to like a spreadsheet mentality. I'm orderly by nature."

"Ha! I'm a vegetarian, and I like boiled rutabagas, but I sure wouldn't want to live on them for the rest of my life. Now you take that writer friend of Charles's. On second thought, I'll take him. That's one side of beef even I wouldn't turn down."

Rory didn't want to talk about Kane. She didn't want to talk about Charles, either, but she felt compelled to defend him. "Just because a man doesn't sit on the floor and tootle a flute and get high with his friends doesn't mean he's dull."

"Oh, Bill and Sunny don't do that anymore. Sunny's developed these allergies, and Bill's had so many hassles with the FDA ever since he went legit, he doesn't dare."

"Thank the Lord," Rory said reverently. "If Mrs. Banks ever thought... What did y'all talk about last night before we got there, anyway?"

"You. Us. Our family trees, our medical histories—you know, the usual uptight, uptown drill. She wanted to know who we had in the Revolutionary War, and if Grandma Truesdale was UDC or DAR."

Rory groaned. Sunny's views on war were—eccentric, to say the least.

"Then the cook, Mrs. Behappy or something like that—"

"Mountjoy. Carrie Mountjoy."

"Whatever. She fixed us some kind of a casserole—I think it was rice and pickles and cabbage, I'm not sure, and then we went out to the backyard to see where your wedding is going to be committed. I told her she needed some compost around her roses, and she told me about her slugs, and Sunny told her about pans of beer and leaving a few weeds around her flowers so the poor bugs would have something to eat, and everything was as peaceful and nice as rice pudding."

"You mean Fauna didn't offer to strip and dance for the wedding?"

"She was sleepy. Her last gig was this private party, and we picked her up right after she got changed."

Rory groaned again. "Yes, well, I'd just as soon Charles and I said our lines before a justice of the peace and let it go at that, but he said his mother wouldn't hear of it, so—"

At Misty's commiserating I-told-you-so look, Rory clenched her teeth and plowed into the kitchen cleanup.

Misty tied on an apron to help. "Bill must've been looking for something to eat that wasn't coated with sugar and soaked in preservatives."

"Then he should've picked another boarding house."

They had just put away the last opened canister when Fauna shoved the door open, yawned and beamed at them. "Hmm, I'm sort of glad we came, after all. Nice scenery. I thought it was going to be a dead bore, but Sunny said we'd better all come early to help support your morals. She kept getting these weird vibes."

"She means moral support," Misty said as the most beautiful of the Hubbard sisters yawned again and scratched her stomach.

"I know what she means. Do you want something, Fauna?" Rory reached for a clean cup from the dish drainer.

"Mmm, what's on the menu? If you're offering me a slice of that delicious hunk of yours, I'd have to say yes."

"You mean Kane?" Rory asked, her eyes widening.

Fauna just laughed. And after a moment of surprise, Misty laughed, too. Rory glared at first one and then the other. She planted her hands on her hips and began tapping her left foot in what her sisters used to call Rory's rattlesnake dance. "All right, you two, just stop that!"

"I'm sorry, Rory, it's just—" Misty began.

"Too perfect!" finished Fauna. "Talk about Freudian!"

"What do you bet Sunny's already hit on it?" Misty asked.

"Scorpio, you think?"

"With those sizzling bedroom eyes, he's got to be."

"Do you two creeps *mind?*"

They sobered up then, and Fauna offered to lend Rory a red silk garter for her something borrowed, but Rory was in no mood to be placated.

Besides, Charles would have a hissy if he saw her in a red silk garter. He wasn't the kind of man to appreciate that sort of thing, even if she were the kind of woman to wear it.

"Oh, I nearly forgot—Charlie said to tell you he'd see you this afternoon, and we're all going to some club for dinner," Misty said.

"Including your Candy Kane," teased Fauna. On her way to the stove to pour herself a cup of coffee, she executed a stylish bump and grind and then wobbled her way back to the table, not spilling a drop.

Rory glared and then sighed and gave up. Fauna was simply—Fauna. There was probably a better word to describe the way she walked, but for the life of her, Rory couldn't think of it. When Fauna moved, everything wiggled. Shoulders, hands, breasts, hips—the works.

"Do you have to walk like that?" she asked, sighing again. She'd done a lot of that lately.

"Like what?"

"Like a bowl of gelatin."

Fauna pursed her silicone-enhanced lips. "Comes with the territory, I guess. I'll teach you if you think it'll help soften up your Charlie boy. Or do I mean harden him up?"

She grinned with an innocent wickedness. Misty giggled. Rory gritted her teeth. Into that atmosphere Kane sauntered, his white shirt half unbuttoned and his hair still wet from his morning shower. "Mornin', ladies. Am I interrupting something?"

Rory, her face flaming, said, "Not at all. If you want to do me a favor, could you take these two children out to play while I eat my breakfast and organize my day?'' Suddenly she felt a million years older than her two sisters, who were twenty-two and twenty-five respectively, to her thirty. Old and tired and lonely and . . .

Frightened.

Obligingly, Kane led both women out through the back door into the lazy, late-morning heat, and Rory hated herself for hating the fact that he was with them and not with her.

And then she suffered the feelings of guilt that seemed to plague her at every turn these days.

What the devil had she ever done to feel guilty about? Charles had insisted that she invite her family to their wedding, and she'd done it. She had suggested that Kane entertain her sisters, and he was doing it. Charles had said he'd see her this afternoon, and in his arms, maybe she could shed the feelings of guilt and uncertainty and plain old cold feet that had been haunting her day and night ever since he had handed her her engagement ring.

Maybe if he'd put it on her finger—and maybe kissed it and then folded her fingers into her palm, instead of just handing over the box and telling her where he'd bought it in case she wanted to exchange it for something more to her taste. . . .

Rory dressed carefully for her outing with Charles. She wore his favorite dress, a pale blue cotton with white dimity collar and cuffs. She splashed cologne on her throat and dusted face powder over her freckles, knowing full well it would melt off within minutes.

Charles embraced her, and with her arms around his neck, she touched her wrist to see if her pulse was racing.

Oh, well . . . it was too hot to race, anyway.

They drove to a small riverside park, and Charles left the engine running for the air conditioner. Heat or not, Rory would have preferred to get out and sit on the grass, to feel the warm currents of air eddying off the muddy Yadkin River. She was not her parents' child for nothing.

"It's a wonder my whole family didn't pile into the back seat and come along to see the sights," she said, only half joking.

"Kane'll keep them entertained. He and Fauna seem to have hit it off right well. It might be a good idea if you'd have a word with her, Aurora. Kane's a—well, I mean, he's a thoroughly decent man, of course, but with women— What I'm trying to say is that your sister's pretty young. I'd hate to see her hurt."

"Fauna?"

"Is that really her name?"

"It really is. Charles, is your—that is, are you— Well, what I'm trying to say is, I'm not sure your mother will be happy living with us." She didn't want to talk about her family. She especially didn't want to talk about Kane and Fauna.

"It was Mother's home until Suzanne and I were married. I can't very well tell her she's not welcome, Aurora. She wouldn't understand. She'd be hurt."

Rory's shoulders drooped. She told herself that Charles was a kind man. Considerate sons, she had read somewhere, usually made considerate husbands. "I suppose so."

"You'll be glad of her help once school starts, you know."

There was that, of course. Charles had never once objected to her going on with her teaching, and really, she was a good teacher. She had a way with children. Someday she hoped to have children of her own.

"I told Kane to have the girls back by five. They'll want to have time to get ready for tonight. Fauna said she was in the entertainment business."

Strangling on a burst of laughter, Rory looked to see if he was serious. Her sister had been known to tell people in all seriousness that she was a professional kootch dancer, just to watch their reactions.

He was serious. She stared at his flawless profile. Charles Banks really was a very handsome man. His features were perfect, not at all like—

"Yes, well—" she said, ducking her head to study her chewed-off fingernails. "She is. An entertainer, I mean. Charles, do you love me?"

He looked as if she'd hit him with a dead fish. "Aurora, that's an idiotic question. Would I have asked you to marry me if I didn't care for you?"

"I didn't ask if you cared for me, I asked if you loved me, because if you do, you have a funny way of showing it."

"Aurora, I think you're overtired. That's why I asked Mother and Eve to take over the arrangements."

Rory started to protest, but Charles held up his hand. She couldn't help but notice that it was softer and smoother than her own. "Aurora," he said gently, "we're not a pair of starry-eyed youngsters. I know this is the first time you've been married, but my dear, you're thirty years old. Surely you've had time to realize—a sensible, educated woman like yourself—that words like love are highly overused. Care, respect— those are the important ingredients in any successful relationship. Similar backgrounds..." Here he frowned just slightly, but Rory, her eyes blinded with tears, didn't see it.

"Well, I suppose that will work itself out," he murmured. "By the way, your father mentioned an umbrella policy last night, and I'll tell you frankly, I'm amazed that he doesn't have one. In his business, a man can't have enough insurance."

"I think I'd like to go home now, if you don't mind," Rory said very quietly.

"Well, of course, my dear. Your head's hurting, isn't it? You've had a lot of headaches just lately."

Rory had had a lot of stomachaches just lately. She never had headaches. But she didn't bother to set him straight.

Seven

In the basement of the big, square Banks house, the ancient hot-water system fought a losing battle to keep up with the demands of the female guests. On the second floor, Kane, who had chivalrously waited until last to shower and shave, bore the cold water stoically, then scrubbed himself dry with a stiff, freshly ironed towel. He marveled at a mentality that insisted on ironing all linens, down to the last dishcloth.

Rory and Maddie Banks sharing a household?

No way.

Rory and Charlie Banks sharing a bed?

Over his dead body!

"Kane, are you decent?" Charles called softly through the bedroom door a few minutes later.

"Yeah, ready in a minute."

Charles opened the door and walked in, resplendent in a pale gray suit that looked like every other suit he had worn for the past dozen summers save for minor variations in cuffs, lapels and coat buttons.

Kane glanced up. He grimaced. "Charlie, don't do it," he said.

"Do what? Kane, it's a quarter of. Can you hurry it up a bit?"

Kane swore quietly. This was a rotten time to throw a monkey wrench in the works. He hadn't even planned what he was going to say, much less which one he was going to say it to first. For a man who made his living with words, he wasn't even up to rough-draft standard.

Dammit, he had as much integrity as the next guy. He'd always considered himself an honorable, decent sort. Well, hell—at least he'd never dealt off the bottom of the deck!

The thing was, it didn't add up. He'd known this woman less than a week. He had known his ex-wife for nearly three years before he'd married her, and that match hadn't even survived the honeymoon.

Besides, Charlie was the one who wanted a wife. Kane didn't need one. He had his life-style down pat. He had a small house outside the historical district, close enough to the water so that he could walk out on the breakwater and fish for blues whenever the notion struck him. Or he could just pick up and drive for days with no particular destination, until he'd winnowed the chaff out of his brain. A wife, he didn't need. A woman—well, hell—he was no eunuch!

But when the woman in question was Aurora Hubbard—midnight porch scrubber extraordinaire, modeler of beeswax, teacher of children, junk-food junkie, shy, zany, trying-her-damndest-to-be-square Rory,— then he couldn't just take her to bed, thank her kindly for the pleasure and then drive off into the sunset alone.

Charles sniffed the air and opened the west window another few inches. There were room air conditioners in most of the major areas, but this had been a box room before it had been turned into a makeshift guest room. "Kane, I really appreciate your being such a good sport about giving up your room last night. It just never occurred to me that Aurora's entire family would turn up this way—certainly not so early. Mother and I had figured on making reservations for them in town."

Kane fastened his cuff links. Normally he didn't wear links. Normally he didn't even wear a shirt, not when the temperature and the humidity both hovered around the low nineties. It was only one of the advantages of his carefully chosen life-style. "Interesting people," he observed absently, still trying to convince himself that he was an altruist of the first water, with only his friend's best interest at heart.

"That's a polite way of putting it, I suppose. That mother of hers is rather peculiar, but her father—Kane, the man wears beads! What did you think of the sisters?"

"Pretty. Interesting. Different."

"I understand the brown-haired one is a dancer. Pushy little thing! She strikes me as no better than she ought to be."

Kane, jutting his chin before the mirror to knot his tie, grinned broadly. "Yeah? How good do you think she ought to be, Charlie?"

Charles frowned. "You know what I mean. She's some kind of a showgirl. An entertainer, she says."

"You mean like the kind of entertainer that used to shut down the King Fair back when we were kids?"

"It wouldn't surprise me one bit. Can you believe it? A sister of Aurora's in *that* profession and openly admitting it?"

Kane managed to keep a straight face, but it wasn't easy. "Charlie, get real. Bumps, grinds and visible skin are what passes for dancing on your average junior talent show these days. The same raunchy stuff that was against the law back when we were growing up. Face it—times change, sex sells and money talks."

"Yes, well—what I meant was they don't seem like the kind of people Aurora would have come from. She's not at all like that. She's—"

"She's what, Charlie? Are you sure you even know who she is?" Kane's voice was casual, but there was nothing casual about the searching look he sent his friend as the sound of muffled feminine laughter drifted down the upstairs hall.

"What kind of question is that? Of course I know who she is. Kane, you're not really going to wear that tie, are you?"

Kane patted the gaudy rayon tie he had bought off the street in the Keys. It was just offensive enough to suit his taste. "Nice, huh? I always had a weakness for coconut palms and sunsets. Would you like one like it for a wedding present? I've already given Rory hers. A pair of sneakers."

Charles's mouth opened and closed silently a few times, and then he pulled his cuff back and frowned at his watch. "I can appreciate a joke as well as the next man, Kane, but would you mind getting your coat? I'm sure the ladies are ready by now, and I made the reservations for seven."

"You do know she's all wrong for you, don't you, Charlie?" Kane reached for the natural-linen jacket he'd previously tossed in the back seat of his car. He shook his head. "Don't do it, man. Don't ruin two lives."

Or maybe three.

Charles followed him out into the upstairs hall, his black-and-white wing tips ringing sharply on the golden oak floor. "Well, I'll admit her family's not all it could be, but Aurora was raised by a grandmother, under entirely different standards. No matter how she might have started out, she's obviously turned into a decent, respectable woman. She's neat and quiet, and she lives within her means. She—"

Kane halted at the top of the stairs, dark eyes blazing. "Damn your bones, man, you're not hiring a housekeeper! We're talking about the woman you're planning to marry! The woman you're planning to take to bed! The woman who's going to take your seed into her body and make you a baby—a whole flock of babies!" He broke off, swearing. "Ah, hell, Charlie, let her go before it's too late."

Three steps down, Charles looked back at him. "I think you must have been drinking, Kane. I'm sorry for you, but if you have a problem, maybe you'd better seek—"

Kane laughed harshly. "Yeah, you could say I have a problem, but it's not drink."

With a last suspicious look, Charles measured his treads down the rest of the stairs and waited by the front door. "Mother's offered us the use of her station wagon. I'll take the Hubbards."

But Kane wasn't done yet. "You do know you're going to make each other's lives pure hell, don't you? Rory's not the woman you think she is. With you she's like a butterfly in a jar, beating her wings against the glass. After a while, she'll stop trying to fly, and when that happens, she'll die."

Charles frowned at his watch and then frowned at the upper landing. "You're talking nonsense. You always did have a peculiar imagination."

"Right. And you had none. But Charlie, it's not my imagination. Rory's overreacting to something that happened when she was a kid. Fauna told me about it, and it explains a whole lot. The reason she went into teaching, the reason she appears to be the kind of woman you think she is, is that she's trying her damnedest to be somebody she's not."

"Absurd. Are you sure you don't want to borrow one of my neckties?"

"Dammit, it's not absurd, either, and no, I don't want to borrow one of your undertaker's specials! Rory thinks if she lives by her grandmother's rules, she'll be safe, but it's eating her alive! And you're just encouraging her to become another Maddie Banks!"

By now Charles's face was dangerously red. "Hush! I'll not have you speak of my mother that way! I don't know what that young woman told you, but she's just trying to make trouble. She's jealous because Aurora turned out to be a decent, law-abiding—"

"God, you don't have a clue, do you? Tell her it's off, man. Before it's too late, do yourself and Rory both a favor and set her free." Disgusted with himself for losing his temper and blowing his whole case, Kane turned to stare at the brass umbrella stand, while Charles stared out the distorting lens of a panel of beveled glass beside the broad front door.

"Hey, do we have to hire a couple of escorts, or what?" Eve appeared at the head of the stairs wearing white silk slacks and shirt with an ornate turquoise-and-silver belt. "Darlings, you have six hungry women on your hands, and that's downright dangerous!"

Charles strode down his front walk, around the hedge and up the walk next door, past Rory's elderly sedan with the rust-primed fender where she'd lost an argument with a pickup truck last month. She was waiting until her first paycheck to get it finished.

The other three Hubbards were waiting. Charles looked over his fiancée's dress, nodded his approval and escorted them out to the station wagon, leaving Eve to ride with Kane.

Rory watched as the couple drove off. Sunny watched her watching and smiled. She nudged Bill. In the back seat of the station wagon, Fauna smiled at Misty, who winked, and Peace dug out her nail file and smoothed a rough edge.

Rory told herself it might seem like jealousy she was feeling, but it wasn't. Eve was strikingly beautiful. She was sophisticated, she had a flawless complexion, not a freckle in sight, and evidently she had remembered Kane better than he'd expected her to.

She sighed and scratched her third finger, left hand, where a rash had appeared earlier that day.

Fauna was in a wicked mood. Rory watched her teasing Charles, watched Charles's ears turn bright red, and frowned. Her mind a miasma of loose ends and half-finished details, she managed to murmur an occasional response to Sunny's chatter about dreams and auras and gristmills and the lovely hand-painted silk gown she had brought for Rory to be married in.

Appalled, she said, "But Sunny, I already have a dress."

"But this one's special. I designed the material just for your wedding, and I only finished sewing on the top skirt this afternoon. It's layered gauze with hand-painted trees, wildflowers, birds and butterflies in the softest colors imaginable, and—''

''But Sunny—'' With a sinking feeling, Rory thought of Kane standing in a dress shop, his dark face grave, one hand on his hip, the other hand stroking his jaw as she modeled one after another outfit. She thought of her precious honey-colored silk—sourwood, not buck-wheat—and how Kane had looked at her when she had emerged from the dressing room wearing it. At that moment, something had happened to her heart that had affected her eyesight. For the longest time, she hadn't been able to tear her gaze away from his.

She thought of some of his more outrageous re-marks and how she had giggled when he'd referred to the flouncy, rose-colored silk the clerk had produced as the embarrassed flamingo costume. She had laughed more that day than she had laughed in years.

But this was Sunny, and Sunny loved her, and Sunny had made her a special wedding dress. She sighed. ''I'll try it on when we get back.'' She twisted her ring. What would Charles say when she showed up wearing one of her mother's free-form, floaty, hand-painted crea-tions? Kane would've understood, but Charles?

Fumbling in her purse, Rory found a roll of antacid tablets.

Was there still a foreign legion? Did they accept women? Did a woman have to be French to volunteer, and how long did it take to get a passport?

Eve and Kane were waiting when they reached the club. Eve was laughing and hanging on to Kane's arm like kudzu on a pine tree. Nor did the pine tree seem to mind being strangled, Rory noticed. She forced a bright smile. "That's a wonderful necktie," she said, and to no one's surprise, Sunny echoed the sentiment.

Turning to Charles, who was frowning at Sunny's layered handkerchief hemline, Rory continued to smile. If he thought that was wild, he was in for a major shock. Wait until he saw her in one of her at-home costumes, complete with foot jewelry and jade nostril stud.

Before they were led to one of the big round tables near the French windows, Rory managed to take Misty aside and threaten to put a curse on her firstborn if she so much as raised an eyebrow when the dinner orders were placed.

"Down, girl. I assure you, I'm housebroken. Eat your dead animals, see if I care, but we all know who has stomach troubles and suitcases under her eyes from not being able to sleep."

"Just remember," Rory hissed. "Not one word, no matter who orders what!"

They placed their orders for drinks when the menus were brought, with the Hubbards agreeing to sample a local wine that was making quite a reputation for itself. Eve ordered a gin and tonic, Kane seltzer with a twist, and Rory milk.

So far, so good. And then Kane said, "Charles—your permission to embrace your woman?" And while Charles was still wordlessly opening and closing his mouth, he led Rory out onto the dance floor, where two other couples circled slowly in a small clearing among tables.

"You've been looking harried," Kane said as he slipped his arms around her and drew her close.

"Misty says I look like hell. Is harried better or worse than hell?"

"Different in degree, maybe." Kane's voice was a raspy purr. His warm breath against her cheek raised goose bumps down her entire right flank, and Rory rested her forehead momentarily on his shoulder.

"I am a little tired. I hate to think of starting school in less than a month."

"That's not the only thing that's supposed to be starting in less than a month."

"You mean marriage."

Kane was tempted to tell her he meant something else entirely, something neither one of them had bargained for. Was she as aware of what was happening between them as he was? It couldn't be all one-sided. It was too powerful not to have been generated from two sources.

His arms tightened around her, and her head rested against his shoulder like a bird coming home to the nest. What good did it do to tell himself a decent man didn't steal a friend's woman when the feel of her in his arms, the scent of her in his nostrils, made him forget every principle he had ever claimed to honor?

When the silence threatened to implode, he said, "I like your family."

She raised a startled face to his. "You do?"

Kane laughed, and Rory felt the deep rumble in every cell of her body. How did he do it? How did he manage to affect her physically by simply laughing?

It must be evidence of something lacking in her diet. "Sunny has a dress she wants me to wear."

"She's shorter than you are."

"Not hers. One of her creations. There's this shop in Richmond and another one on the Outer Banks that sells everything she makes."

"Smart woman."

"Mmm-hmm." With Kane's arms around her waist, her hand tucked securely in his big, warm paw, and her head resting on his shoulder, she didn't want to talk about her family or Charles or anything disturbing. If she could just drift a little longer...

"Are you going to wear it?"

"I don't know what to do. I can't bear to hurt her feelings. On the other hand, Charles will hate it."

"What does Rory want to do?" He brushed his face against her hair, and she was glad she had washed it that afternoon, rinsing it in an herbal mixture of Sunny's that added shine and the scent of summer rain.

"I don't know," she whispered helplessly. She let herself drift a moment longer. With Kane's arms around her, her problems didn't seem all that insurmountable.

Problems? What problems? She was going to marry Charles, and her sisters had promised to behave, and in a few more days, Kane would be gone, and...

Kane would be gone.

The pain she felt inside her then was not something that could be cured with a dose of antacid. "Hadn't we better go back to the table?"

"The band's still playing. You're shivering. Are you cold?"

"Kane, please," Rory pleaded. She glanced over her shoulder, half expecting Charles to pounce on her and accuse her of—

Well, of something wicked, anyway. Some impropriety. Some breach of etiquette. Like wishing with every bone in her body that Kane would kiss her again.

Charles wasn't even looking her way. He was dancing with Fauna on the other side of the room, and even from this distance, Rory could see that Fauna was up to something.

The music ended, but Kane didn't release her immediately. His arms tightened, and he said in a rough whisper, "Do you have any idea how much I want to kiss you right now?"

Closing her eyes, Rory groaned. Suddenly, her nice, neat world was falling apart. "Stop it, Kane."

"And if I did, do you know what would happen?" She melted against the warm granite of his body, achingly aware of every hard ridge and plane. A few thin layers of cotton did not a firewall make! "Kane, please don't talk this way."

"I'll tell you what would happen, lady," he said, ignoring her protest. "We'd both go up in smoke, that's what would happen if I kissed you now. Like lightning striking a dead tree. Like flint on steel. Like match to tinder."

"Stop it!" She broke away and glared at Kane, who glared right back at her. Oblivious to the few curious stares, they stood toe to toe, both breathing hard, both pale—Kane's coffee black eyes burning into her tea-colored ones.

Using every shred of self-discipline that had been drilled into her since she was eleven years old, Rory broke the spell. "Kane, I don't know what you're trying to do, but you've got to stop. It—it's not fair, to Charles or to me."

Kane's shoulders sagged, making him suddenly look older than his thirty-seven years. "What about me, Rory?"

"What about you?"

"I'm trying to save you from making the worst mistake of your life."

"No you're not. What you're trying to do is confuse me. You're playing some—some game for your own amusement, and now you've got me so mixed up I don't even know my own mind, and it's got to stop. Kane, just leave—me—alone!"

She told herself she only imagined the pain that sliced through his eyes. Men like Kane—hard men, men of the world—didn't feel pain over someone they had known less than a week.

"You're worried about Charles, aren't you?" she asked, more gently. That was it, of course. He thought she was all wrong for his friend, Charlie. "Kane, I'll be a good wife to him, I promise you. It may not be a fairy-tale romance, but we'll do just fine. Charles and I are old enough to know what we want, and—"

"What do you want, Rory?" Kane broke in softly, his eyes moving over her face so intently she could actually feel them.

"Oh, well—I want—that is, Charles and I want—Well, neither of us is getting any younger, and Charles said married men live longer. He said there are statistics to prove—"

Kane uttered a creative string of oaths, and Rory winced. "If that's what you want, it's your funeral—ah, make that *wedding*," he amended with a bitter twist of a smile. And then he walked off and left her there, and Rory, her face now flaming, blindly made her way to the ladies' room, where she popped two antacids, splashed cold water on her face and then painted a bright slash of coral across her lips.

Somehow she got through the rest of the evening. Misty didn't organize a protest march against cow killers and lobster murderers. Fauna didn't dance on any tables, although twice she dragged Charles onto the dance floor with her, and wiggled her arms around his waist up under his coat. Once she rubbed her nose against his necktie and deliberately tickled his chin with her hair, and Rory could have spanked her, because Charles *hated* that sort of thing. He didn't care for demonstrativeness of any kind.

At least Sunny didn't offer to read any palms, auras or handwriting, and Bill didn't try to make a deal with the kitchen staff to serve only Hubbard's Heavenly Herbals. All in all, she supposed, it had been a successful evening.

What do you want, Rory? The words kept echoing in her mind.

You! Kane, all I can think of is what it would be like to lie naked in your arms, to feel your touch on every part of my body—to finally know what the rest of the world means when it talks about ecstasy and passion and being singed in the flames of love!

On the ride home, Kane lent Charles his car, and he drove the others, leaving Charles and Rory to follow at their own pace. It was Rory who suggested they pull over halfway home, in the empty parking lot of the Baptist church.

"I haven't had a minute alone with you for weeks," she said.

"For goodness' sakes, Aurora," said Charles, switching on the eleven o'clock news on WSJS, "I just spent a whole afternoon with you. I don't know what you're complaining about."

Neither did Rory. She only knew that something wasn't right. "That doesn't count. We hardly talked at all, and you didn't even kiss me." Reaching over, she switched off the radio midsquawk and said, "Charles, what would you say if I asked you to make love to me?

Now. Tonight, that is. We could go somewhere—to a hotel, maybe.''

"Good Lord, Aurora, what's got into you?"

"That's no answer!" she exclaimed, exasperated.

But it was. In a way, it was exactly the answer she should have expected. Disheartened, she tried again. "Can't we even talk about it? Are you impotent, Charles—is that it?"

"Aurora! I refuse to sit here and be insulted!"

"Because if you are, it's all right. I mean, sex isn't the most important thing in a marriage. Really, it hardly counts at all if two people really like each other and respect each other, and—"

"Aurora, I think the strain of—"

"But we'll probably do it sooner or later. I mean, most married people do, don't they? I mean, if we're not going to do that," she said with a shatteringly brittle smile, "why bother to get married at all? There wouldn't be any children to consider. We could just go on being friends."

Charles expelled his breath in one hard gust. With unaccustomed abandon he reached up and jerked his tie loose from his collar. "It may come as some surprise to you, Aurora, but I'm as normal as any other man. I have the same urges and, I presume, the same capabilities. The fact that I haven't, uh, pressed myself on you so far is a mark of my respect, not an indication of any physical lack on my part. I assure you, once we're married—"

"But why wait? Most people these days don't even wait to get engaged."

"You're asking me to take you into town to a hotel and prove myself to you before you make a commitment, is that it? You want a guarantee that I can, uh, perform my duties as a husband?''

"No, that's not it at all!" Rory cried, wondering how she could explain what she meant—explain her fears, her doubts, to a man who refused to even try to understand.

Arms crossed, Charles faced her in the harsh glare of the church's security light. "My dear, the so-called sexual liberation is over. It proved to be a crashing failure. Now, I've always believed in decent family values, and I thought you did, too. That was one of the things that attracted me to you. In this day and age, a man can't be too careful."

"Oh. I see. You mean it's all right for a man to be experienced, but when it comes to marriage, he wants a virgin bride? Is that what you're saying?"

Much put upon, Charles sighed. "No, that's not— that is, of course I— Aurora, how would you like to face your family tomorrow morning after spending the night with me at a hotel?"

"My family? Are you serious?" Remembering all she had seen and heard as a child—all she had heard about and read about, if not actually seen, since then—Rory couldn't help but wonder if there was something odd about Charles.

Or if there was something odd about her. Oh, how she wished she had never said yes to Charles, never met Kane, never been subjected to all these miserable, conflicting—*urges!*

In his well-modulated voice, Charles went on to say, "How could you face my mother, Aurora, knowing we had acted like a couple of irresponsible teenagers, sneaking around to have sex without even considering the possible repercussions."

The thought of facing Madeline Banks at all, much less after a night of unbridled passion, legal or otherwise, was more than Rory could cope with. How could she sleep with Charles under his mother's roof, with his mother under the same roof? Suddenly it was not only appalling, it was impossible.

"Forget it," she said tiredly. "Let's just go home. I'm sorry I brought it up, it was just—just that—"

"I know, my dear, you don't have to apologize. It's prenuptial tension. We're all suffering from it, even Kane. It's the unexpected upset of having your family piling in on us, I suppose."

Charles didn't mention his own family's piling in on them, Rory noticed, but then, that was different. He was their own. They were his. And soon she would be one of them. Soon she would be his, too.

Oh, God, what have I done? Get me out of this, please, before it's too late!

Eight

Everyone was talking at once. Rory stood in the kitchen doorway, wondering how she had got to this particular point in her life. She wondered whether to go back to bed for the next few years or just to gird her loins, cover her eyes and jump into the fray. Having given up on joining the French Foreign Legion, she considered the possibility of joining a religious order. One of the silent ones.

She had a headache. She *never* had headaches! Her finger itched, and she scratched it absently.

"That creep? Ha!" Fauna had found Rory's secret cache of Reese's Pieces and was talking through a mouthful of peanut butter. "I knew the first time she ever brought him home he wasn't worth diddly. He was even worse than—"

"Rory, where do you keep your measuring cups?"

"A philosophy student! Is that what he said? That jerk was about as deep as an oil slick! Rory, do you have any lemons?" This from Misty. Hot lemon water was her matutinal beverage of choice, family business not-withstanding.

"Bill, if you want your shorts washed, drop 'em in the basket, I'm getting up a load."

At his wife's command, Bill obediently peeled off his rumpled cutoffs, and Rory goggled at his lurid tie-dyed drawers—obviously one of Sunny's less successful experiments.

Head pounding, stomach growling, she reluctantly joined the mob, only to discover that someone had finished off her chocolate milk, and her peanut jar was empty of all but a film of greasy salt.

Sunny held something under her nose. "Sweety love, what's all this mucky stuff in your measuring cups?"

"Beeswax for my—"

"Lord, Rory, you don't actually eat this junk, do you?" Misty held up a cereal box and began reading off the table of contents. "It's nothing but empty calories."

Fauna lunged across the basket of laundry and grabbed it. "Hey, a miracle food! Does this mean I can eat all I want and I won't gain any weight?"

"What are you all doing over here?" Rory asked.

No one heard her, and she repeated it, louder. "I said, what the devil is everybody doing in my house, dammit?" she repeated, louder still.

Dead silence. Every face in the room turned her way. Sunny blinked her thick, colorless lashes and said, "Lovey, are you all right?"

Bill said, "Charlie offered breakfast before he left for the office, but Mrs. Monkjaw doesn't come in until ten."

"Mountjoy," Sunny corrected automatically. "Madeline was busy, too. She has to get her linen closet turned out before the wedding. Did you know she's a Virgo? Sun, moon, Mars and Mercury. Poor woman."

Misty, a wicked gleam in her guileless blue eyes, turned to Fauna. "What were you doing in Charlie's room this morning? I bet Rory would like to know, wouldn't you, Rory?"

But Rory was no longer listening. Very quietly she retraced her steps and closed the bedroom door behind her. Forty-seven minutes later she emerged again, impeccably, if inappropriately, dressed in her honey-colored jacquard suit and her new tan pumps. She carried a hatbox and a small padded mailer in one hand, a suitcase and a battered leather shoulder bag in the other.

She had never got around to shopping for a purse to match her new outfit.

Calmly, she faced the barrage of questions. When they dwindled out, she said, "There's barbecue-flavored pork rinds in the canister marked Flour and candy bars in a whipped-topping container in the freezer, upper left-hand shelf. Help yourselves. I'm going to meet Charles in town. I have something for him. I probably won't be home until sometime tomorrow."

Bill frowned. Misty looked puzzled. Fauna started to protest and then shut up, while Sunny simply smiled her maddening, oracular smile.

Kane took the long way back. He'd been driving for hours. Being in sole control of a few tons of well-behaved hardware seldom failed to clear his brain. Occasionally he borrowed a plane for a few hours when he had something to work out—usually a snag in a plot. This time it was more than an unruly plot, and driving to hell and back wasn't going to help.

Kane had never aspired to be a saint. In the first place it sounded boring as hell. Still, it had come as something of a shock to discover just what a lowdown, unscrupulous bastard he could be when conditions were right. Or, as in this case, wrong. He'd thought he had more character than that.

Last night, between Bill Hubbard, who wanted to talk insurance, and the lineup of women waiting for the two bathrooms, he had managed to grab five minutes alone with Charlie. Granted, his timing had been lousy, but time was the one thing he didn't have.

It had been late. A few of the Hubbards had been a bit too enthusiastic about the local sauvignon blanc, and for some reason, Charlie, the unflappable, had been edgy as Satan on ice.

Of course, that might've had something to do with that miniature Venus panting into one of his ears, while Hubbard was bending the other one about commercial rates and umbrella policies.

Or poor old Charlie might've just had to use the john.

In any case, Kane had corralled him and herded him into the back bedroom, where he'd told him point-blank to forget marrying Rory.

"I beg your pardon?"

"Charlie, listen to me—she's not going to marry you. Don't you see—"

"What I see is that it was a mistake to think you'd changed. You still don't care one iota about other people's property. You still—"

That had blown it right off the stack. "Dammit it, man, she's a woman! She's not a piece of furniture you're buying just because it matches Maddie's front parlor rug! She's alive and real and wonderful, and you're stifling her! She can't even breathe properly when she's with you, for being afraid you won't approve of the way she inhales!"

"Did Fauna put you up to this?"

It was the last reaction Kane had been looking for. He'd started swearing, and by the time he'd managed to convince himself that knocking some sense into the poor stiff could wait until they'd both had some sleep, Charlie had slammed out of the room.

Fauna? The older one, maybe—she was the marrying kind, and she was ready to go on the prowl again. But *Fauna?* That was so far out in left field it was funny!

On second thought, maybe it wasn't so far out. Kane frowned. As a plot device, it was a natural. Almost a cliché, in fact.

By the time he pulled up in front of the Bankses' place again, banners of orange sunlight were beginning to filter through the trees. He'd been driving all night. The key was hidden right where it had always been hidden for the past twenty years. Quietly Kane let himself inside, tiptoed up the stairs and crashed for the next six hours.

Rory had never in her life stayed in a room that cost more than thirty-eight dollars a night. She had never even stayed in a hotel. A schoolteacher learned to be frugal, and hers was a motel budget. A *budget* motel budget! And she'd already spent more on a single outfit than she usually spent in an entire season on clothes.

It didn't matter. She wasn't going to think about it, and when she checked out and used the last of her savings to pay her bill tomorrow, she was not going to regret a single penny.

This was her honeymoon. Her honeymoon for one. There wasn't a blasted underwriters' convention in sight, and she had a king-sized bed all to herself and a Jacuzzi as big as Lake Norman, and she was going to soak and sleep and maybe order another pizza and diet cola and ice cream from room service, and as soon as she could figure out how to operate that gizmo on the television set, she was going to find herself an X-rated movie—or at least a nice sleazy soap opera—and tomorrow she would go home and calmly tell her family that the wedding was off and to please go home.

Sniffling, she dug another gooey slice of pizza out of the box.

It was nearly four o'clock in the afternoon before Kane located her. Five by the time he got there. He'd had the devil's own time tracking her down, even with the entire Hubbard clan and Charles's secretary to help.

"I'm sorry, Mr. Smith, but she really didn't say where she was going when she left here. She gave me a message for Mr. Banks and that was all." He'd tried Charlie's secretary first.

"A message?"

"More like a package, I guess you could say."

"A package?"

"Like a ring box. It was in a padded mailer, but that's what it felt like. Mr. Banks was in conference when Miss—"

"What time was this?" Kane had demanded.

"Eleven-o-seventeen," replied the ever-efficient Mrs. Spainhour.

Kane had sworn fluently in an obscure Middle-East dialect. Dead end. Not a clue! He had already tackled Charles, who had admitted stiffly that Rory had returned his ring with regrets, given notice on the house, which had been rather redundant, as the next tenant had already signed the lease and would take up occupancy on the first of August.

What now? Call in the cops? Get out an APB on a middle-aged, gray, American-made sedan with a rust-primed left front fender?

Torn between laughing, swearing or knocking hell out of the street sign on the corner of Fourth and Main, Kane remembered Charlie's bragging a few nights ago that he'd arranged to have her car repainted while they were in Cincinnati as a surprise wedding gift.

God! No wonder the woman had walked!

"She was all dressed up when she left," Bill had told him that morning.

"She had a suitcase with her," Sunny had said.

"And she did say she'd be back tomorrow," Fauna put in. Her mascara had dribbled down her cheeks. She'd been crying.

She damned well ought to cry, Kane fumed. If Rory had found out that her own sister was putting the moves on Charlie, it was no damned wonder she'd split! The only wonder was that she hadn't jerked a knot in the pair of them before she left!

It wasn't because she was any plaster saint, either. In less than a week, Kane had seen beneath that placid freckled surface to the real woman underneath. Seen more than he'd wanted to see—more than he could ever forget.

It took a handful of calls to pin her down to the town's best hotel, and then he'd hit another brick wall. Because, while the hotel was perfectly willing to put him through to her room, they refused to tell him the room number. He could have called, but then she might have run again, and he'd be right back where he started.

Instead, he'd placed a call to his agent, launching into his demands with no preamble. The man, after all, owed him a favor. "Ross? Kane Smith. Look, I need—"

"Kane, where the hell are you, anyhow? I've been calling every five minutes since day before yesterday! They said you'd checked out—" An excellent agent, Ross Klingman was inclined to hyperbole.

"I'm in North Carolina, a place called Tobaccoville, and I need—"

"Oh, sh—! Listen, man, how long will it take you to get yourself out to the Coast? I think we've got Costner interested, but unless we can go to contract before—"

"Ross, will you just shut up and listen? I need you to make a call for me! Now here's the number and here's what I want you to do."

"It'll cost you. How long will it take you to hitch up your mule and get out of Tobacco Road to somewhere where they've heard of the Wright brothers' little experiment?"

"Very funny. I'm a hell of a lot closer to PTI than you are to JFK. Look, if I promise to be in New York in three days, will you just shut up and make this call for me? It's a matter of life and death." Kane, too, had been known to exaggerate for effect.

"Listen, sweetheart, I want you at LAX, and I want you there tomorrow, latest, and I don't give a sweet damn in hell if your grandmother's giving birth to triplets! Do we have deal?''

They had a deal.

An hour later, Kane, wearing his incognito gear, which made him stand out like a sore thumb, strode into the lobby of the hotel on Fifth Street and demanded the service his agent had ordered. "My—ah, secretary, Miss Hubbard, should've checked in two days ago. What floor did you put us on? I never stay in a room above the fifth floor."

"Miss Hubbard? Why—uh, we have a Miss C. A. Hubbard, but she only arrived today."

Kane raked a hand through his hair in a gesture that had been known to make strong women grow faint. "Damn," he said softly. "She must've missed her flight out of Heathrow. Now we'll never get caught up." And then, as if making the best of a rotten deal, he said, "Okay, okay—not your fault. Just send up my bag, a pot of coffee and today's *Times,* London and New York. Oh, and if anyone from the media asks, you never heard of me, understood?''

"Uh—would the *Journal* and the *News and Observer* do? We don't get the London papers, and the only *New York Times* we get is Sunday's, and it's already sold out."

Kane looked at him over the rim of his glasses until the man swallowed visibly. "Yes, Mr. Smith, right away, Mr. Smith. Coffee, *Times,* no reporters—and, uh—Mr. Smith, could I have your autograph? It's for my mother." The desk clerk hadn't a clue as to who this guy who called himself Smith really was, but he didn't intend to take any chances on missing an opportunity.

Kane swallowed his laughter, thankful for the reflective surface of his dark prescription glasses. He scrawled his name illegibly across a sheet of hotel letterhead, nodded to the bellman and strode across the lobby.

Dismissing the bellman outside the door with a tip large enough to do the job, but not so large as to raise suspicions, Kane let himself into Rory's room. Glasses in one hand, battered flight bag in the other, he stared at the figure in rumpled cotton pajamas sitting cross-legged beside a half-empty pizza box in the middle of about two acres of quilted bedspread. The air conditioner was set on Arctic Blizzard.

And she'd been crying. Snail tails of shiny tears ran silently down her speckled cheeks. Wearing the same outfit she'd had on the first time he'd laid eyes on her, she gave up staring at the weather channel and turned her red-rimmed amber eyes toward him, and suddenly Kane felt like crying, too.

"Rory?" he murmured gruffly. "Honey?"

"That's not fair," she said, and pulled a crumpled tissue out of her pocket. "How did you find me? Please go away."

Kane dropped his bag, tossed his glasses onto a nearby table and crossed to the bed. She turned back toward the TV screen. The tip of her short, elegant nose was red. Her lips were pale. There was a smudge of tomato sauce on her chin, and she was freezing. She had goose bumps on every freckle.

Kane reached out and adjusted the thermostat, and then looked at her some more. His adrenaline had peaked, leaving him with a postmission letdown. So he'd found her. Now what?

Hell, he flogged himself—just look at her! She was a mess! Kane had known hundreds of women who were far more beautiful than Crystal Aurora Hubbard. He'd even married one of them. He'd known a lot who were

probably smarter, too—not to mention more successful. Depending, he amended, on how you figured suc-
cess.

What did this one have that had got under his skin
and into his dreams? He'd gone around in a state of half
arousal ever since he'd kissed her that first time, and
that hadn't happened in many a year!

"Lady, what is it with you?" he muttered. "I've
passed my magnet over hundreds of shiny new alumi-
num cans without so much as a dip. But along comes
one lousy rust-speckled scrap of tin and I'm stuck!"

He shook his head, pulling out his handkerchief as he
crossed to the bedside. Leaning over, he carefully wiped
the pizza sauce off her chin. "What are we going to do
about it?" he asked gruffly.

Rory took a deep breath and began reassembling her
dignity. It might have been an easier task had she not
been wearing the same old ratty pajamas she'd been
wearing the first time she had ever bumped into Kane
Smith. It wasn't as if she didn't have a perfectly lovely
nightgown right there in her suitcase. She'd brought
along her entire trousseau, such as it was, even going so
far as to wear her wedding finery in some sort of sym-
bolic gesture. Only by the time she had eaten her way
through three quarters of a large kitchen-sink pizza and
a double-chocolate sundae with extra nuts and extra
cherries, she was in no mood for fancy new clothes,
even if she could have squeezed into them.

She looked him in the eye. "Go away. I don't want
you here."

"You're lying."

"Is your ego really that inflated?" Her eyes were
burning, and she pinched her thigh, vowing silently to
pinch even harder if a single tear escaped. She was no

whiner. She'd made up her mind and done what had to be done, and that was the end of it.

"Honey, what's wrong? Let me help."

"I can't imagine why you think I need help. I'm perfectly fine."

"Sure you are," he said gently. And then he continued to stand over her, like a solicitous hawk, guarding his own.

"All right, so I made a mess of things! I can't do anything right, but at least it's done now!"

Personally he thought she'd done a pretty good job, once she'd come about onto the proper heading. Kissed off Charlie, walked out on her family—declared her independence. He was proud of her, and surprisingly, he wasn't at all surprised. "What is it you think you can't do?" he asked indulgently, teasing a little—wanting a lot more than he dared claim just yet.

"Anything. Everything. Oh, I don't know! I wanted to use the Jacuzzi, but I've never used one before, and I was afraid I'd electrocute myself, and I can't figure out how to work this blasted TV set, and I've always hated digital clocks, anyway!" She swallowed hard, looking everywhere but at the man with the shaggy dark hair and the crooked smile, the man in the sinfully sexy black jeans and raw linen shirt that had to be custom tailored.

"What did you want to watch? I'm pretty good with things like TV sets and digital clocks. I've even mastered the Jacuzzi."

"Bully for you," she said sullenly. "I didn't invite you on my honeymoon, and I'm not in the mood for company, so if you want to leave, feel free."

"Honeymoon?" Kane eased himself down onto the foot of the bed. It was too close for Rory, about half a mile too far away for Kane.

Ruthlessly she wiped her eyes and crammed the wet tissue back in her pocket, where it called attention to the fact that she wore nothing at all underneath. Deliberately, Kane studied the quilted pattern of the bedspread until he had himself under control.

"It seemed like a good idea," Rory muttered. "Well, I thought as long as I wasn't going to go to Cincinnati, I might as well take myself on a vacation right here at home before school starts." She drew in a deep, shuddering breath, wishing she'd brought the box of tissues from the bathroom. She couldn't even think *that* far ahead! "I just needed to get away by myself so I could sort things out. Can you understand that?" she demanded.

"What happened to Cincinnati?"

"You already know," she said with a suspicious glare.

"Yeah." He glanced at the empty ice-cream bowl and the half-empty pizza box and helped himself to a slice. It was cold, but then he wasn't particularly squeamish. "You always eat this way?" he asked after chewing and swallowing. The sauce was terrific, the crust tough. "No wonder you've got stomach troubles."

"There's nothing wrong with my stomach."

"I know."

"But you just said—"

Kane replaced the half-eaten slice in the box. Reaching for her hand, he examined the red rash on her third finger, left hand. "I've always known what ailed you, Rory. I was beginning to think you might not figure it out in time."

Sighing, Rory surrendered the last scrap of defensiveness. She nodded. "Me, too."

"You want to talk about it?"

"There's nothing to talk about."

"You discovered—?" Kane prompted. He waited, not pressing her.

"I discovered that I didn't really love Charles, so it wouldn't be fair to marry him. I could never be the kind of woman he deserves."

"No," Kane said thoughtfully. "I don't suppose you could."

She sneaked a quick glance at his tanned, irregular features—the crooked nose, the crooked mouth, those wonderful eyes that made her feel warm and cold-shivery at the same time. "I really pitched a fit over his mother, did he tell you? At least I said in the note I gave his secretary along with the ring that I didn't think Mrs. Banks would be happy living with us."

"Wise decision." He deliberately kept his expression under control, but it wasn't easy.

"Kane, did you ever wonder where you belonged?"

Kane nibbled on his full lower lip. His teeth, Rory noticed absently, weren't crooked. They were perfect—except for one chipped corner. "I don't know that I ever thought much about it."

"I think about it a whole lot," she said wistfully. The room was warming up, but she still looked cold. Huddled there in the middle of the king-size bed, she looked like an unhappy child and a desirable woman all rolled into one delectable, if untidy, package.

Kane figured he'd better deal with the former before he got down to dealing with the latter. Rising, he left her and disappeared into the bathroom. Rory heard the water running. She picked a slice of olive off the pizza and nibbled on it, then reached for her used tissue to wipe the smear of sauce from her fingers. It was soggy.

Hell, damn, spit! She couldn't even manage a decent honeymoon for one.

The sound coming from the bathroom changed just before Kane beckoned to her from the doorway. "Madam's bath is ready."

"Whose what is *what?*"

"Temperature's perfect, and I promise, you won't be electrocuted. Trust me on this, will you? I've always been a whiz with anything mechanical."

From the other room Kane listened to the splashing noises. He pictured her dropping her pj's on the floor and stepping one foot in at a time. He pictured her lowering her delectable little rump into the swirling water, closing her eyes and leaning back until the steamy water tickled her rosy nipples. He pictured—

"Sweet Saint Peter," he muttered. Getting up, he crossed to the window and stared at a pigeon on the roof of the Benton Convention Center. Until she was joined by a second pigeon, at which time he swore, jammed his hands into his hip pockets and began to pace.

Fifteen minutes later Kane rapped on the bathroom door. "Hey, look alive in there! I've got a pot of hot coffee for me, a pot of hot chocolate for you, a bottle of wine if you need any Dutch courage, and there's a big, thick bathrobe hanging on the back of the door."

"How do I get out of this thing? What do I need to do?"

"You really want me to come in and show you?" One word of invitation, and you wouldn't see him for his contrail.

The word didn't come. "Just climb out, wrap up and come on out, I'll take care of everything." He ought to be canonized for this.

Twenty minutes later Rory was leaning back against a mountain of pillows, a glass of wine in her hand and a cup of neglected hot chocolate on the table beside her. She felt warm and relaxed and secure, and if the wine was partly responsible, at least she had sense enough to enjoy it while it lasted.

Thoughtfully Kane twirled the stem of his glass between his blunt-tipped fingers. Thoughtful by nature, he decided on the subtle approach. "So what the devil ever made you think you and Charlie could get along as next-door neighbors, never mind husband and wife? You'd have driven each other nuts in a month's time!"

So much for subtlety. He was discovering that patience wasn't his long suit. That thick terry-cloth robe, for instance, didn't help. It was miles too big. The neck gaped open, giving him a glimpse of one sloping breast, right down to the line of demarcation where the freckles faded out. Add to that the fact that she smelled like soap and sunshine and sweet, warm woman, and her eyelids were beginning to droop, and it was all he could do to hang on to his good intentions.

"Why'd you do it?" he asked finally.

"My grandmother, I guess. She was—she had—I suppose you could say she had very high standards. She would've approved of Charles."

"For you?" Kane scoffed. "Not if she really knew you. Not in a million years."

Kane refilled her glass, and then somehow Rory was telling him about her childhood, about growing up as free and wild as a weed, about how scary freedom could be when one could only sense the dangers and wonder at the boundaries. "There was a lot of talk about love, but I'm not sure people always liked each other very much. Sometimes I wanted to say, he's lying, or she's not what she pretends to be, only I couldn't, because we were all one big family. We all belonged to each other, but..."

She frowned, and Kane found to his discomfort that even the furrows on her freckled forehead could turn him on. He shifted to a less-revealing position and tried to think about something nonincendiary. Dammit, he was trying to be her friend, and all he could think about was burying himself in her sweet, hot depths and dying there!

"You know, it was strange. I used to wonder if I'd been adopted, or stolen from my real parents. Of course I know now that most children wonder about things like that at one time or another in their lives."

"When you're Sunny's age," Kane rasped, "you'll look exactly like her. She's a beautiful woman."

Rory smiled her thanks. "Still, I used to feel sort of—oh, I don't know—dispossessed." She sighed and sipped. When she licked her lips, Kane shut his eyes. Speaking of possession, he thought hotly...

With a sigh of quiet surrender, he kicked off his shoes and joined her on the bed. Leaning back against the pillows, he propped his arms behind his head and tried to look cool and unaffected. Tried to tell himself she was just a woman he happened to meet, a friend of a friend. Tried to tell himself he wasn't so damned crazy in love with her he couldn't function.

They talked about her move to Kentucky to live with the grandmother who had never really forgiven her own daughter for running away when she was sixteen. "I'm still not quite certain they're legally married."

"I doubt if it matters, except to the IRS."

"And to Mrs. Banks." She smiled. And then she laughed aloud. "I reckon she's glad I'm no longer a threat to Charles. I don't think she liked me very much."

Kane grinned. "Welcome to the club. Rory, why'd you take up school teaching?"

"Grandma was a schoolteacher. She retired soon after I went to live with her. She had arthritis pretty bad. And I missed Misty and Fauna and Peace. And, too, I liked the idea of a disciplined life. There's a certain security in something as structured as teaching. A place to belong. Does that make any kind of sense?"

"It makes a lot of sense." Especially to a child who started out life in a hippy commune, he added silently. "Did it work?"

She sipped her wine and tilted her head thoughtfully. "Sort of."

With that, he had to be content. Maybe no one ever really belonged anywhere. Belonging was a state of mind—one he hadn't given a lot of thought to lately.

He did now. "My father was in the air force," he said after a while. "I never knew him. He died in a training mission before I was born. My mother had just started at Duke on a scholarship. They planned to be married on his next leave, but he crashed, and she was five months pregnant with me, so she dropped out and took a job as a research assistant. It didn't pay a whole lot."

Somehow Rory's hand had found its way inside Kane's. Turning her fingers, she squeezed. "I can imagine," she said.

He shrugged. It had been years since he'd even thought of all this, much less talked about it. His wife had never asked about his childhood.

"Her brother helped out when she got too far along to work. She stayed with him until after I was born, but his wife made it pretty uncomfortable, I gather, so as soon as she was able, she moved to King and got a job in an office. When I was five, she switched to waitressing. It paid a lot more and allowed her to be home during the day. We moved into Maddie Banks's bungalow and lived there until Charlie and I went off to school. End of story."

"You told me your mother—"

"She died a few years ago. She'd had a mastectomy, but she'd evidently put it off too long." He said it calmly, just as if he hadn't cried himself raw during her illness and afterward.

"No other family?"

"No other family." Until this moment he'd never particularly thought about the lack. Hell, everybody went through moments of loneliness.

But this was different. That half-nostalgic, half-melancholy feeling that had begun to creep up on him just lately—it was more than loneliness. And it was strangely absent whenever he was around Rory Hubbard. She was like sunshine spilling in through the windows of his soul, lighting up corners that had been dark so long he'd grown used to the darkness.

She sipped her wine. Her head moved a fraction of an inch and came to rest quite naturally against his shoulder. It seemed the most natural thing in the world that his left arm should go around her shoulder and she should snuggle up against him, her bent knees resting against his thigh.

"I don't usually talk so much," he said almost apologetically.

"Neither do I," she confessed. "At least, not about—personal things."

"Like why you were sent to live with your grandmother?"

She was silent so long he thought she wasn't going to respond. Something told him that this was important. Somewhere in here was whatever it was that she'd been hiding from, all these years. It just might be the single thing that had nearly driven her into a disastrous marriage.

"I've never told anybody this before," she said in a quietly determined voice. "But once there was this man—I was eleven, and I'd just started—you know—changing."

Kane's hands curled into fists. His voice dropped an octave, into something cold and deadly. "Your breasts had started growing, you mean."

"Whatever," she mumbled. "Anyway, I was uncomfortable around him, but he never actually did anything. It was mostly the way he looked at me. He, um, he smiled a lot."

Kane could well imagine how a certain type of slimeball could affect a sensitive, self-conscious girl. Nor did it occur to him to wonder how he was able to empathize with something he could never have experienced personally. He just did, that was all. With Rory the child, Rory the woman— With Rory fifty years from now, a lifetime of memories secured behind the facade of age.

When he began to swear under his breath, she covered their clasped hands with her free one and peered up at him. "Kane, nothing happened. Honestly. I'm not stupid, you know. The night it happened—that is, nothing really did, but the night I'm talking about, when all the grown-ups were high and Ian was sleeping over, all us kids were sharing the same room. We usually did. So when I woke and found him there with his hand on my—well, anyway, I elbowed Peace, and she woke up the others, and he left. The next day Bill and Sunny went to town and made a few calls, and pretty soon after that they took me to live with Grandma."

Feeling Kane's tension, she forced a chuckle. "Talk about a change of climate! From skinny-dipping in the creek to a tub bath every day. I hated it at first! We had gooey oatmeal every morning, and I had to clean off my plate on account of the poor starving orphans."

"How did you adjust?" It was more a play for time than anything else. Kane was having problems with Rory's nearness. For the life of him he didn't understand how a mild interest a week ago could have grown into something so damned powerful it scared the living hell out of him.

But it had. And now that he'd found her—now that she was free—he was going to try to take it one cautious step at a time, give her a chance to catch up.

The trouble was he'd never been a particularly patient man.

"How did I adjust?" she repeated with a warm, sexy chuckle that pulled his throttle all the way out. "I'm beginning to think I didn't." She grinned up at him, and his heart did a couple of lazy barrel rolls. "Unless you consider thirty-year-old, slightly schizoid virgins to be well adjusted."

Nine

The silence lasted for a century. Rory's face began to burn. Tangled in the thick sash of the terry-cloth bathrobe, her fingers twisted nervously.

"You want to run that one by me again?"

"I can't believe I said that," she whispered.

"The schizoid part or the other?"

"Both. Neither." She began to edge away from him, and without making an issue of it, he hauled her back. At least with her head buried in the curve of his shoulder, she didn't have to face him.

What a thing to say! Now she knew why she never drank alcohol. No tolerance. Inhibitions down the drain.

"I'd better have some coffee," she mumbled, freeing herself in an attempt to reach past him.

Kane's arms came around her again, and he caught her to him, off balance, breast to chest, face entirely too close to face. "You don't need coffee. I'm not sure just what it is you do need, but I have a pretty good idea." Kane knew exactly what she needed. She needed him, is what she needed. She needed a man who loved her enough to let her go free, but who needed her enough so that she would always have a place to belong. A man who was patient enough to wait if she wanted to wait, but who hoped to hell she didn't, because he was going to explode in about two minutes and counting!

"Rory—honey, listen to me," he rumbled against the top of her head. She was breathing through her mouth. He could feel the steam heat on the front of his shirt. He didn't want so much as a shadow between them, but he couldn't think of a graceful way to get them both undressed without being obvious about it.

This was going to take a little more finesse than usual. A *lot* more finesse than usual. Because for the first time in his misspent life, Kane knew the difference between making love and having sex, and it wasn't just sex he wanted from this woman.

At least, it was—but he wanted one hell of a lot more from her besides. And he wanted it for one hell of a lot longer than one sweet tumble would take.

"You're trembling," Rory said, twisting in his arms to look at him.

"You noticed," he said dryly.

"You're not cold?"

"Hardly. Honey, stop wiggling before you hang yourself. Aren't you uncomfortable in that thing?" He was. All her twisting around had pulled the thick bathrobe off one shoulder, giving him a breathtaking view of a shoulder, a clavicle and half a breast. Any more strain on his zipper and they were going to need flak jackets.

"I'm not really schizoid, you know. At least I don't think I am. It's just—"

Carefully Kane lowered her to the bed and leaned over her. Placing a finger over her lips, he said, "I know. I'm no shrink, but I think I know what your trouble is. Trying to be all things to all people never works for long. All it does is bend you out of shape and make you mean as a cottonmouth."

"Do you think I'm mean?" She looked so hurt he couldn't stand it. Slowly he shook his head, his face no more than a foot above hers as she stared up at him from those clear-as-a-mountain-stream amber eyes.

"No, lovey." Her mother called her that. Because her mother loved her, too. "No, you're not mean and you're not crazy, and you're about not to be a virgin anymore if I have anything to say about it."

Kane could actually see her heartbeat in the trembling of her breast. Easing himself onto one elbow, he placed his hand over it. Not cupping, not cradling—not even caressing. "Easy does it, love. We'll go as far as you want and no farther. I'll do my very best not to hurt you."

Her eyes were enormous. This close, her freckles melded into one caramel-colored blur as he closed in on her lips. *Won't hurt you... never hurt you... lovely woman, love you, woman...*

At the first touch of his tongue, Rory fell apart. Somehow the sash to her robe was dangling over the edge of the bed, the two enormous flaps spread open, and Kane was pressing her down onto the cool sheets, his body hot and hard above her own. She was beyond rational thought. Her senses told her truths she had known for a thousand years—that the slightest brush of this man's fingertips had a profound effect on her body.

That just thinking about him, much less looking at him—much less *touching* him!—did things to her that she'd thought were beyond the realm of human possibility.

Her pulse raced out of control. Her trembling thighs moved restlessly. Her fingers dug into the resilient muscles of his back in an effort to draw him closer. To draw him inside her—to make him a part of her, indistinguishable, yet wonderfully, oh so wonderfully, different!

His mouth twisted on hers, firm, yet so incredibly soft. The taste of him went straight to her bloodstream, more intoxicating than the headiest champagne.

This had never, never happened to her before. When she felt his hand on her breast, his fingertip shaping her hardened nipples, she gasped; only with his mouth making love to hers, it came out as a muffled sort of "Mmm-mmm."

"Many clothes," she murmured when his mouth left hers and moved to her throat. And then she arched her throat as she felt him nibble his way down the sensitive tendon along the side.

Kane fumbled with the buttons of his shirt. "You're sure?" he panted, and with one hard jerk, he managed to pull the thing free. Buttons rolled silently on the pale carpet as he undid his belt buckle and fumbled at his fly.

His briefs were yellow. With tropical fish on them. He was embarrassed. In Key West they hadn't seemed so gaudy, but now he wished he'd stuck to something less flamboyant. She would think—

"Your underpants are pretty," she said, and he closed his eyes and laughed helplessly. Stripped down to his skivvies, he'd been called a lot of things by a lot of different women, but pretty wasn't one of them.

"Sweetheart, if you think these are something, wait'll you see the ones with the bluebirds and cabbage roses."

But the joke was over; because Kane had rolled onto his side, and what she was staring at wasn't any tropical fish. It was him. For one split second he considered pulling the sheet up over them, but he didn't. This was the testing ground. Either she trusted him or she didn't. Biology and anatomy courses aside, there was a hell of a lot more involved here than the mating of two adults of opposite genders. But it was a beginning.

"Rory?" She managed to drag her eyes away from *it* and lift them to his. "Sweetheart, I promise you we won't do anything you don't want to do, but you have to know that I—that is, you— Well, the thing is, if you want me to leave, you'd better tell me now, because in a little while it's going to be damned near impossible."

Her eyes widened. He could read her fear, her uncertainty—her need—as well as he could read the Do Not Remove tag on the pillow. She was aching for him and afraid to admit it. Afraid of all the old taboos her grandmother had instilled in her—afraid of a half-remembered childhood incident. Afraid, maybe, of all the terrors that stalked the night.

"Listen, you do know what happens, don't you? I mean, no one can get to be your age, or even half your age, without knowing, uh, what goes where. The mechanics."

She nodded, her eyes never leaving his. Kane suspected she was afraid to tear her gaze away for fear of where it would go next. He felt an overwhelming tenderness come over him. The combination of tenderness and horniness was totally new to him. So he said,

"In a way, I guess I'm almost as much a virgin as you are."

Her feet freezing, her face flaming, Rory dragged her gaze over his shoulder. There, in the mirror on the opposite wall, she saw a back that tapered from broad, tanned shoulders down to a narrow band of colorful cotton. Beyond the brightly colored fish extended a pair of lean, muscular legs that were covered with dark hair. He had narrow feet. High arches. Sunny would have said it was a sign of something or other.

Curiously she studied the other person in the mirror—or at least, the few visible parts. There was a pair of freckled legs with thin ankles and rather knobby knees. Over the broad, tanned back she could see a naked shoulder, a flushed face and a mop of tangled, sunstreaked hair.

Dear heavens. She was naked in a hotel room with a decadent bathtub, in bed with a man she had known less than a week, and she was about to make love to him. Oh, yes she was, too. If she'd suspected before that her wits were addled, she was certain of it now.

"I know how it's done—well, probably not everything, but at least the missionary position and—well, I know it's supposed to hurt the first time, too, but since that doesn't keep anyone from wanting to do it—a lot— then I guess it can't be too bad." The words came out in a little rush, and Kane thought his heart would burst.

"Then listen and pay attention, my little darling, because I'm going to complete your spotty education. The, uh, so-called missionary position has its merits, but for the first time... Well, there are differing theories as to which is the best way."

"Don't you know?" She was lying half under him, her hands on his shoulders.

"Not—everything. Rory, I'm not pretending to be a virgin. What I said—well, I meant, for the first time, I'm with someone I care one hell of a lot about, and it's—it's just different. I want to take care of you. I want to pleasure you so that you'll know what all the hubbub is about." And so you'll want me again and again, until we're too old to do more than cradle each other in our arms and share the warmth of a lot of sweet memories.

He wanted to make those memories with her. But most of all he wanted right now to make love to her until neither of them had the strength to get out of bed. And then rest and do it some more.

He was trembling again, braced to hold back his own pleasure until he had seen to hers. Before and after, so that maybe the pain in between would be forgotten.

"It starts here," he said, placing a hand on her head. "And then it goes here—" The hand stroked down her body, coming to rest on the pale floss between her thighs. Rory gasped. Her thighs clamped his hand, and he withdrew immediately. "And then," he said, sliding his hand slowly over the flat plain of her belly, the hollow centering her rib cage, to rest over her left breast, "if you're very lucky, it winds up right here. In your heart. Or the part of your soul the heart's supposed to represent. Do you understand?"

"I think so."

"Repeat after me, it starts in the mind." It had never started there for him before. "Next it zones in on the libido and related parts." As in, want it, figure out how to get it and enjoy it while it lasts. At least it had always been that way before. "But in a few rare and wonderful cases," he whispered unevenly, "when the right two people have found each other, it ends up right here. The heart. And points beyond." And he cupped her left breast in his hand and leaned over to place his open mouth on the pink thimble-shaped crest.

Lightning shafted through her. She clutched the sides of his face, her fingers gripping his thatch of warm, vital hair. She could feel his ears—not too large, not too small—perfect. Just as he was. With his crooked nose and his crooked smile and his irregular face, he was so perfect she still couldn't believe her luck.

Because inexperienced or not, Rory was no fool. Kane wanted her, and not only wanted her, he cared for her. Maybe he even loved her the way she loved him.

Before she could explore the possibilities, his kisses moved down over her, searing her flesh along the way, making her wild with a need she only dimly understood. And then she cried out, "Kane, what are you doing to me? Ahh, please, I can't bear it! Something's happening to me! Oh—oh—*ohhhh!*"

She moaned and twisted as, with skill, patience and great tenderness, Kane set her on fire and then fueled the flames again and again. He was hanging on to his own control by a thread that was unraveling rapidly.

But she loved him. He was sure of it. She trusted him, and it was going to be all right!

By the time Kane moved over her again, the yellow field of tropical fish lay somewhere on the floor. Rory was utterly drained, her eyes half-closed, her lips parted. She felt as if she were pulsating with a bright pink light.

"Sit up," Kane ordered.

"Can't. No bones. Limp."

"That's wonderful, sweetheart, the trouble is, I'm not."

He lifted her until she flopped over his shoulder, and then shifted them about until she was sitting astride his thighs. Her arms hung loosely over his shoulders, her head sagged back, like a top-heavy blossom on a too slender stalk. She was smiling. Beaming.

"This is me, Rory." He took her hand and placed it on him, and ground his teeth as her soft little palm began to explore. There was a small foil packet on the bedside table. He wished now he had put the damned thing on first, because her touch was driving him wild!

Through clenched teeth, he said, "Enough show and tell. Give me a minute, love, and then we'll go to the next stage, all right?"

She nodded, and he thought at that moment she would have agreed to anything, because he had pleasured her so well. It made him feel proud. It had been his pleasure, too, and almost his undoing. He hadn't come so close to losing control since he was about fifteen.

"Now," he said a few moments later. "This is the hard part."

And damned if she didn't touch him again. "You mean this?"

Kane uttered a pained gasp of laughter. "Yeah, sweetheart—that. Now this is what we're going to do. You're a teacher. You know a lot more than most kids do when they get involved this way, so I don't have to explain what's going to happen to you. But I do want you to know that anytime you want to back out, you can do just that. Get up, get off, walk away. I promise you, I won't cry too long, and I'll still respect you even if you don't go all the way."

But Rory, feeling the soft, glowy warmth starting up again—not that it had ever entirely left—didn't need any instructions. She was, after all, a college graduate. Theoretically, she knew about all there was to know.

Only she wasn't prepared for the strangeness of actually becoming a part of another person—for the strangeness of feeling herself...filled. Hands on Kane's shoulders, she lowered herself gingerly onto that rigid part of him. She was frowning in concentration. Kane was sweating. Once he swore under his breath, and she froze, afraid she had done something wrong.

Really, theory was a lot different from actual practice.

Kane breathed out in a deep, shuddering sigh. "Did I remember to tell you where to ship the remains?" he grated.

Rory had come to the hard part. She knew it. He knew it. She wiggled her hips experimentally and felt the stinging, pulling sensation. And then, closing her eyes, she lifted her hips and sat down, hard. She bit off a cry of pain, and Kane groaned and gathered her so tightly against him she couldn't breathe.

"Ah, sweet, sweet Rory. Wait a minute, will you? Don't move. I think it'll stop hurting pretty soon."

It had already stopped hurting. She felt full, but it wasn't just a fullness of body, it was a fullness everywhere. Very deliberately, Kane took her face between his hands and smiled into her eyes. And then he kissed her, and somehow, they were all turned round, and she was lying on the bed and he was over her, and then he started to move—slowly, at first, and then faster...

This time again, she burned to a cinder, and this time again, it was every bit as wonderful, only different. And the difference was wonderful, too. Not until a long time later, after Kane had arched and cried her name in a guttural groan, did she realize she was smiling.

More of a smirk, actually, but close enough. She snuggled in his arms, once he shifted onto his side, and fell instantly asleep.

Kane woke several times in the night. He gazed down at her in the light that came in through the window from the streetlight below. He'd majored in math at school, raced through to a degree in three years' time so that he could join his father's branch of the service and fly. After the flying, the alternate thrill and boredom of life in the service, had come the other—the writing, the restlessness, the seeking something and never quite knowing what it was.

Until he'd found it. Thank God he'd had enough sense to recognize it and to go after it, no holds barred!

Quietly, wanting to wake her and take her again— knowing it was too soon, that she'd be sore—he got up and fumbled in his flight bag until he found his notebook. After showering, he got dressed in the cabbage roses and bluebirds and his spare shirt and sat down to write.

Rory slept on, and if she smiled now and then in her sleep, the smiles weren't wasted. Kane caught every one of them, writing a few lines and staring at the woman on the bed a few feet away.

Finally, without reading it over, he placed the note on her bedside table, anchoring it with the half-empty hot-chocolate cup. When she woke up he'd be well on his way, wishing he were right back in her arms.

He wished to hell he could just trash the whole deal, but he owed Ross. He might need to call in a few more favors before too long.

He took one long look, bent over and kissed her and whispered softly, "Lady, I don't know what it is you're packing, but it's powerful stuff.'' He shook his head and stood up, reluctant to leave, knowing that the sooner he went, the sooner he could be back. He had come through Scuds, heat-seekers and several tons of AAA, only to be brought down by a second-grade schoolteacher with freckles and knock knees and a way of laughing that could melt stainless steel.

In a few hours, Kane told himself, she was going to wake up and stretch and wonder where he'd gone, and he wouldn't be here to reassure her.

But she'd read his note and she would know. And the next time he saw her, they could start talking commitment. As in permanent. As in my place or yours, or anywhere in between, so long as it was forever.

Ten

Rory was roused by the sound of a persistent buzzing. "A'right, a'right," she muttered, slapping the table beside her where her alarm clock usually sat. The noise persisted, accompanied by the clinking of china. She opened one eye. Light spilled into the room from the open draperies, but it was an unfamiliar light. Not the cool kind that bounced off a shaggy fescue lawn, but the warm kind that might bounce off a nearby brick wall.

It was an unfamiliar room, in fact. She sat up, ignoring the mess she'd made on her beside table, and realization began to creep in on her. She looked around for the telephone. It had to be here somewhere. The darned place had three, including one in the john!

By the time she padded, naked and barefoot, to the gold-and-ivory instrument on the French Provincial table, it had stopped ringing.

"Hell, damn, spit," she mumbled. Dragging a corner of the sheet around her to cover her nakedness, she dropped onto a rose damask chair and tried to focus her mind. Yawning, she scratched her elbow.

Kane. Dear Lord, what had she gone and done? And where had he disappeared to? And if he was truly gone, then why? She couldn't have imagined it all, not in her wildest fantasy.

By the time she had stood under a lukewarm shower, head and all, for ten minutes, she had thought her way back to the beginning. Back to finding herself suddenly fed up to the eyeteeth with Charles and Madeline and the whole squabbling flock of Hubbards, not to mention tired to death of trying to be all things to all people.

Trying to be all things to all people . . . Who had said that?

Kane. He'd said a lot of things. You'd think when a man and a woman had laid themselves wide open—heart, body and soul—one of them would at least have the common courtesy to hang around long enough to wish the other one good-morning. At the very least.

She thought some more. About the things they had done last night. Things that had changed her forever, and him not at all. About things they had said and a lot of things they hadn't said. Such as I love you with all my heart, and will you marry me and spend eternity with me. Ordinary, everyday little courtesies like that.

She felt raw all over, inside and out. She hurt and was determined not to. It was her own fault. What kind of woman walked out of the arms of one man and into the arms of another? Never in her wildest dreams had she thought she could do something like that.

Only she had, hadn't she? Not exactly out of Charles's arms, but nevertheless . . .

Something had happened to her the moment she had first laid eyes on Kane Smith. Crazy or not, she had fallen in love with the man. He'd probably seen it written all over her face, because she'd never been good at dissembling. Seen it and taken advantage of it, and she could have sworn that the man she loved would never in a million years go off and leave her without so much as a thank you, ma'am.

Only he had, hadn't he?

Actually Kane had probably been more the seduc*ee* than the seduc*er*. He certainly hadn't mentioned love, not in so many words. In her ignorance she had interpreted the look in his eyes as love, when it had obviously been no more than plain, old, garden-variety lust. The kind her grandmother had warned her about. The kind that had led Sunny to run away from home at sixteen and live with a man who might or might not be her legal husband, even now, and produce four—count 'em, four—bouncing baby girls.

Lust. Or at the very most, what her grandmother had grimly referred to as Free Love, which wasn't free at all. Mere hours later, Rory was beginning to suspect it carried an exorbitant cost.

For a long time she sat there, staring morosely at a scratch on the leg of the elegant table. She stared at the phone awhile, too, wondering who could have called her. No one knew where she was. Except Kane, of course. But why would he call when he'd been right here and could have said what he had to say in person?

Unless he was ashamed to. Unless he was afraid she would try and seduce him again. If he thought he'd been compromised, he might just grab his pants and light out, before she woke up and started talking about preachers and rose-covered cottages.

She cried for a little while, because when a woman's been debauched for the first time in her life, she deserves that much, at least. And then, being sensible by nature, she got up and put on her silk jacquard wedding suit and twisted her hair, still damp, into a lopsided roll up the back of her head, anchoring it with the few hairpins she could locate. Carefully she made the bed, straightened the bathroom and grimaced at the mess on the bedside table. The chocolate goo hadn't leaked onto the carpet, thank goodness. She rinsed out the cup and replaced it on the tray. The hotel's gold ballpoint pen and scratch pad were ruined, as was something that looked like a note. Probably the bill for room service.

Holding it by one limp corner, she dropped it in the waste basket. Whatever additional charges she'd incurred during her stay, if they didn't show up on her bill downstairs, she would leave her address and they could mail her a statement.

Forcefully wrenching her mind away from a past that couldn't be changed, Rory gathered up her few belongings, repacked them in the brand-new suitcase she had bought for Cincinnati and gave one final glance around the room. So much for that, she thought, head held high, even if her chin did show an unfortunate tendency to wobble.

She looked longingly at the phone, as if she could will it to ring again. It had probably been a wrong number, but what if it had been—? What if he—?

But it didn't ring, and she couldn't afford to hang around on the gossamer wisps of a fast-fading dream. Checkout time was noon, and she'd had about all the honeymoon her budget would allow. Resolutely she picked up her bag, closed the door quietly behind her and headed for the elevator.

* * *

The van was still there. It had been too much to hope they'd be gone, relieving her of the necessity of a lot of messy explanations.

Not that she had to explain anything. She had said all she needed to say to Charles in her note, and that was the end of that. Actually he'd probably been relieved once he'd gotten over being embarrassed. But then emotion of any kind always embarrassed Charles. And one of the things she had discovered last night was that she was a lot more emotional than she would ever have believed. Not to mention a lot less practical.

Whatever it was that she was—the product of a grandmother who'd been the daughter of one Methodist preacher and the wife of another, and of a pair of hippies-turned-yuppies—at least she knew now that she was her own person, answerable to no one for the way she chose to live her life. Of all the things Kane had given her, that much, at least, was hers to keep.

"I'm back," she called out from the front door.

Sunny emerged from the kitchen, trailing sweet potato vines, a Mason jar in her right hand and a pair of scissors in her left. "Sweetie love!" she cried, throwing wide her arms and slinging water across the living room rug. "I felt sure you'd come to your senses in time! With Venus transiting your Uranus trine your—"

"Sunny, please." Rory dropped her bags, embraced her mother and stepped back. "No transits and trines for a little while, all right? What I need is a cup of coffee and some cereal and peanuts and chocolate milk, but first I want to get out of these clothes and into something comfortable. Where is everybody?"

"Oh. Well, there's this health food store at the mall, so Eve and Peace took Bill shopping with them. Misty's showing Maddie how to make a compost heap, and Fauna..."

They had reached Rory's bedroom by then. Sunny had left the anemic sweet potato vines on the kitchen table, along with some turnip tops, carrot tops and what looked like a small heap of grapefruit seeds. "I was doing your plants," she explained, which was about as specific as Sunny ever got about anything except a few of the more esoteric sciences.

"Where's Fauna?" Rory asked as she stepped out of her skirt and into a faded pink chambray tent dress. "She hasn't gone back to Richmond, has she? I wanted to talk to her about something."

Not Peace, although she had been married twice, nor Misty, who'd had one live-in boyfriend for nearly six months before he left her for the peace corps. Fauna was the expert. She knew about man-woman things. She would know exactly how much of what happened last night was real and how much was wishful thinking.

"Yes, well—I suppose you'll know sooner or later." Sunny beamed her thousand-watt smile. "That's a lovely suit, did I tell you? Too structured for a wedding, but it would have done nicely as a going-away outfit. It's sort of romantic, don't you think? Going-away clothes? There's something sweet about all those old-fashioned fifties things."

"Mother—*Fauna?* If she's done something awful, you may as well tell me, because I'll hear about it, anyway."

"Well, I wouldn't say it's exactly awful. I mean, it might be embarrassing, but really, lovey, we knew all along it was inevitable. I mean, she *is* a Taurus, after all, and he's a Capricorn, and with her moon plunked smack dab on top of his—"

"Moth-er!"

"Oh, all right, all right, but you did ask me."

"I asked you where Fauna was."

"And I'm trying to tell you," Sunny said in a reasonable tone of voice that sounded remarkably like Grandma Truesdale. "Fauna's in North Wilkesboro. Charles has this major client there, and—"

"You mean she went with Charles?" Rory herself had never been invited along on one of Charles's business trips.

"Well, there's this nice restaurant where they serve—"

"Fauna and *Charles?*"

Sunny shrugged. "I tried to tell you. Certain configurations can produce an almost instantaneous attraction. Of course, I'm not entirely sure it isn't more a case of karmic recognition, but then who's to say it can't be both? I mean, if an entity chooses to be born under a certain set of circumstances and a particular planetary influence because—"

But Rory was no longer listening. Fauna and Charles. Her little exotic-dancing, bone-lazy, easygoing sister and uptight, buttoned-down Charles William Edward Banks III. Or was that Edward William?

Three days later life had settled down into a fairly even rut. Charles and Fauna had gotten back in the small hours of the morning, and while nothing more had been said, Fauna had mentioned a dancing school in Winston-Salem she'd been meaning to look into.

And Charles smiled a lot.

And if Rory didn't exactly smile, at least she didn't cry quite so much, except for late at night, when there was no one around to hear. So what if she woke up aching in her heart and soul and a few other empty places? At least her stomach no longer hurt. Her ring finger itch had healed with no more than a slight red scaliness, but even that was fading, thanks to the gunky mixture of chickweed, spikanard, golden seal and olive oil Bill had sent her as soon as he got back to Richmond.

She was almost done with her packing. She still hadn't found another place to stay, which was irritating, since she needed to be settled before school started. Ironically she could very well have stayed where she was except that Charles had already leased the bungalow to someone else.

She would miss the front-porch swing, but not quite so much now that the wisteria had been chopped back to the trunk. Sighing, she scribbled mail, paper, phone!?! on the back of an envelope and tucked it under the edge of a flowerpot. And that was another thing... her plants.

It was half past "Hee Haw" and a quarter to "Masterpiece Theater." Rory watched them both and saw nothing incongruous about it, and even if she did, she no longer cared—when she heard the sound of a car on the roadside gravel in front of her house. Curious, she went to the door. The screen was hooked, and she switched on the bug light on the front porch.

Suddenly her heart swelled to bursting. "Don't be foolish," she whispered. Kane was long gone, and she hadn't heard a word from him, nor did she expect to. He knew the wedding was off, so there was no reason for him to come back to Tobaccoville.

There was a dark, low-slung car parked in front of her house. The interior light came on, but before she could see more than a flicker of movement, a door opened and a tall, familiar figure was momentarily silhouetted against the distant lights of town.

Rory squeezed the doorframe until her fingers ached. "Kane?" she whispered.

"Rory?" If she hadn't known better, she would have thought he sounded hesitant. But there was nothing at all hesitant about that sexy, loose-limbed stride. He took her front steps as if there was not the least doubt of his welcome, and before Rory could ask the first of the questions that logjammed her brain, she was in his arms.

The same incredibly sweet mouth she had dreamed of over and over came down on hers. The same strong arms crushed her to him as if to weld her to his lean, hard body. The same two hearts pounded together, escalating want into hunger and hunger into an urgency that quickly reached flood stage.

"God, I missed you," Kane muttered against her throat. He had swung her up into his arms and was shouldering his way inside before she could catch her breath to protest. "Where the hell have you been? I've called a hundred times, and some idiot keeps telling me the number is no longer in use!"

"It's been—I left—that is, I told them I was moving by the first, but the computer misunderstood and cut me off too soon."

"Never mind, I'm here now," he said, and setting her on her feet beside her bed, he kissed her again. It took a long, long time, because there was so much to say that couldn't be said with words. Fiercely at first and then more gently, Kane made love to her mouth. Without words, he spoke of anxiety, of heart-deep loneliness— of a fear that he had imagined it all and an even greater fear that she wouldn't be there when he got back.

"I almost chartered a plane before the ink was dry on the contract, but the studio was able to get me a direct flight within the hour. God, that drive from the airport in Greensboro, though—!''

Unable to help herself, Rory lifted her face to his again. Reasons could wait—reasons for leaving, reasons for returning. All she knew was that Kane was back, and sensible or not, she loved all that he was or had ever been or ever would be.

And he knew it, without the need for words. He kissed her as if he would draw the very soul from her lips. He kissed her tenderly, as if to soothe all the pain and doubts he had left behind when he'd rushed away. And then he murmured against her cheek, ''I didn't tell you, but you knew, didn't you? My note—I guess I was afraid to put it in writing. Crazy, huh, from a man who makes his living by writing?''

His note? What note? And what difference did it make, because he had come back to her, and he was here, kissing her until she could hardly stand, unbuttoning her shirt and sliding it off her shoulders, and—

''Kane, what are you doing?'' she gasped when he slid the satin straps of her bra down her arms and shoved the thing around her waist.

''You can't guess? You've forgotten lessons one through seven already?'' Cupping her breasts in both his hands, he lowered his head to kiss the pouting tips, and then he simply stared at them and at her, as if he had never seen a woman before.

''How can you make me feel this way?'' Rory whispered.

''I don't know,'' he said simply. ''I don't know how you make me feel the way you do, or why I haven't been able to get you out of my mind for a single minute, ever since I saw you backing your way across your front porch, scrubbing and sighing in the middle of the night.''

Drawing her into his arms so that her naked breasts were crushed against his hard chest, he kissed her again, slowly and very thoroughly. At that moment there was nothing he wanted so much in all the world as to be here with this woman, doing precisely what he was doing, which was kissing her with all the love and loneliness and longing he had saved up over thirty-seven years of hard living.

But it wasn't enough, and they both knew it wasn't enough, and soon Kane's clothing followed Rory's to the floor, and she was in his arms on the lavender-scented white sheets of her own virginal bed.

This time it was real. This time it was no king-size, Jacuzzi-enhanced, wine- and pizza-inspired fantasy.

There was no nervousness, no uncertainty. She opened her arms to him, and he came to her the way she had dreamed it a thousand times. Only this was no dream. It was right, and they both knew it without the need for words. It was there in Kane's coffee-dark eyes as he gazed into Rory's amber ones and lowered his body to hers.

She was ready for him. She had been ready for him all her life—ready and waiting, only she hadn't had the good sense to know it until it was almost too late.

Feeling his thrusting masculinity at the gate of her womanhood, she reached down and touched him. He knew so much more of her than she did of him, and suddenly, she wanted to know all there was.

Kane jumped. "Sweet Saint Peter, what are you trying to do to me?" he gasped through clenched teeth.

"You can see, and I can't. I—I'm curious. Do you mind?"

"Sweetheart, if you want mirrors on the ceiling and an illustrated guidebook, you can have it, only it's been nearly a week, and I'm not sure I can hold out while you finish your education." Kane shut his eyes and braced himself to withstand the tentative exploration, but the feel of her small, firm palm surrounding him was almost more than he could bear. Then, elbowing aside her arm, he eased himself down until his throbbing erection was crushed between her palm and her soft belly, praying he wouldn't embarrass himself before her curiosity was satisfied.

In desperation he rolled over onto his side and brought her with him. Reaching down into the furnace between their two bodies, he found her and began an exploration of his own.

Rory caught her breath. Her hand on him grew still, and gratefully Kane eased himself away. He'd had a 30mm gun jam on him once in the heat of battle. Every damned circuit breaker had popped, and it had been touch and go until they'd got back to base.

That was the way he was feeling now. Fully loaded and about to burst! "Rory—sweetheart—"

His fingers moved slowly on her soft petals. He heard her shuddering gasp, caught the sexual flush on her cheeks and knew a moment of pride unlike anything he had ever known before. This was his woman. He could do this for her—something no other man had ever given her. And selfish or not, he knew a secret pleasure at the thought that she was his alone. Made to love him, made to be loved by him until death did them part. And if there was a beyond, then that, as well.

They came together on a high peak and climbed higher, still. Climbed until both of them soared free and then glided slowly, gently back to earth, thoroughly spent, totally content.

A long time later Rory awoke to find Kane propped on his elbow, smiling down at her. She smiled back and said dreamily, "Can't you sleep?"

"I've been thinking."

"I'm afraid to ask," she said, but she wasn't. Not really. Sunny had told her, before she'd left, that everything would work out the way it was supposed to, and Sunny, for all her flakiness, was seldom wrong about things like that.

"You ever think about moving to New Jersey? You'd like Cape May."

"I'm under contract."

"No problem. So'm I, and I guess mine's more portable than yours. What if we find ourselves a place around here with plenty of room for a year or so and then think about trying somewhere else? Or if we like it here and want to stay, then that'll work, too."

"Are you always so agreeable?"

"Only when I get my way."

Rory smiled. She had a feeling that Kane's way was going to be her way, but even if her way gradually became his, she doubted seriously that either of them would even notice.

* * * * *

Fifty red-blooded, white-hot, true-blue hunks from every
State in the Union!

Beginning in May, look for MEN MADE IN AMERICA!
Written by some of our most popular authors, these
stories feature fifty of the strongest, sexiest men, each
from a different state in the union!

Two titles available every other month at your favorite
retail outlet.

In September, look for:

DECEPTIONS by Annette Broadrick (California)
STORMWALKER by Dallas Schulze (Colorado)

In November, look for:

STRAIGHT FROM THE HEART by Barbara Delinsky
(Connecticut)
AUTHOR'S CHOICE by Elizabeth August (Delaware)

You won't be able to resist MEN MADE IN AMERICA!

Silhouette Books has done it again!

Opening night in October has never been as exciting! Come watch as the curtain rises and romance flourishes when the stars of tomorrow make their debuts today!

Revel in Jodi O'Donnell's STILL SWEET ON HIM—
Silhouette Romance #969
...as Callie Farrell's renovation of the family homestead leads her straight into the arms of teenage crush Drew Barnett!

Tingle with Carol Devine's BEAUTY AND THE BEASTMASTER—
Silhouette Desire #816
...as legal eagle Amanda Tarkington is carried off by wrestler Bram Masterson!

Thrill to Elyn Day's A BED OF ROSES—
Silhouette Special Edition #846
...as Dana Whitaker's body and soul are healed by sexy physical therapist Michael Gordon!

Believe when Kylie Brant's McLAIN'S LAW —
Silhouette Intimate Moments #528
...takes you into detective Connor McLain's life as he falls for psychic—and suspect—Michele Easton!

Catch the classics of tomorrow—*premiering* today—
only from ▼ *Silhouette*

WOLFE WAITING
by Joan Hohl

This big, bad Wolfe never had to huff and puff and blow down
any woman's door—scrumptiously sexy rookie officer Jake
Wolfe was just too tempting and tasty to leave outside in the
cold! But then he got hungry for answers from the suspicious
lady who wouldn't let him two feet near her. What was a big,
bad Wolfe to do?

Huff and puff *your* way to your favorite retail outlet before
Wolfe Waiting—Book One of Joan Hohl's sexy BIG, BAD WOLFE
series—is all gobbled up! Only from Silhouette Desire
in September....

SDBBW1

SILHOUETTE® Desire®

DIANA PALMER
IS BACK!

and bringing you two more wonderful stories filled with love, laughter and unforgettable passion. And this time, she's crossing lines....

In August, Silhouette Desire brings you NIGHT OF LOVE (#799)

Man of the Month Steven Ryker promised to steer clear of his ex-fiancée, Meg Shannon. but some promises were meant to be broken!

And in November, Silhouette Romance presents KING'S RANSOM (#971)

When a king in disguise is forced to hide out in Brianna Scott's tiny apartment, "too close for comfort" gets a whole new meaning!

Don't miss these wonderful stories from bestselling author DIANA PALMER. Only from ▼ Silhouette®

DPTITLES